Altar Ego

Anne Sorbie

Altar Ego

Gender, Property and the Cult of Marriage

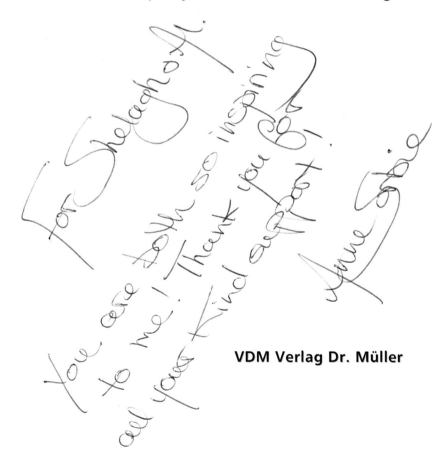

VDM Verlag Dr. Müller

Imprint

Bibliographic information by the German National Library: The German National Library lists this publication at the German National Bibliography; detailed bibliographic information is available on the Internet at
http://dnb.d-nb.de.

Any brand names and product names mentioned in this book are subject to trademark, brand or patent protection and are trademarks or registered trademarks of their respective holders. The use of brand names, product names, common names, trade names, product descriptions etc. even without a particular marking in this works is in no way to be construed to mean that such names may be regarded as unrestricted in respect of trademark and brand protection legislation and could thus be used by anyone.

Cover image: www.purestockx.com

Published 2008 Saarbrücken

Publisher:
VDM Verlag Dr. Müller Aktiengesellschaft & Co. KG , Dudweiler Landstr. 125 a,
66123 Saarbrücken, Germany,
Phone +49 681 9100-698, Fax +49 681 9100-988,
Email: info@vdm-verlag.de

Produced in Germany by:
Reha GmbH, Dudweilerstrasse 72, D-66111 Saarbrücken
Schaltungsdienst Lange o.H.G., Zehrensdorfer Str. 11, 12277 Berlin, Germany
Books on Demand GmbH, Gutenbergring 53, 22848 Norderstedt, Germany

Impressum

Bibliografische Information der Deutschen Nationalbibliothek: Die Deutsche Nationalbibliothek verzeichnet diese Publikation in der Deutschen Nationalbibliografie; detaillierte bibliografische Daten sind im Internet über http://dnb.d-nb.de abrufbar.

Alle in diesem Buch genannten Marken und Produktnamen unterliegen warenzeichen-, marken- oder patentrechtlichem Schutz bzw. sind Warenzeichen oder eingetragene Warenzeichen der jeweiligen Inhaber. Die Wiedergabe von Marken, Produktnamen, Gebrauchsnamen, Handelsnamen, Warenbezeichnungen u.s.w. in diesem Werk berechtigt auch ohne besondere Kennzeichnung nicht zu der Annahme, dass solche Namen im Sinne der Warenzeichen- und Markenschutzgesetzgebung als frei zu betrachten wären und daher von jedermann benutzt werden dürften.

Coverbild: www.purestockx.com

Erscheinungsjahr: 2008
Erscheinungsort: Saarbrücken

Verlag: VDM Verlag Dr. Müller Aktiengesellschaft & Co. KG , Dudweiler Landstr. 125 a,
D- 66123 Saarbrücken,
Telefon +49 681 9100-698, Telefax +49 681 9100-988,
Email: info@vdm-verlag.de

Herstellung in Deutschland:
Schaltungsdienst Lange o.H.G., Zehrensdorfer Str. 11, D-12277 Berlin
Books on Demand GmbH, Gutenbergring 53, D-22848 Norderstedt
Reha GmbH, Dudweilerstrasse 72, D-66111 Saarbrücken

ISBN: 978-3-639-01840-0

Acknowledgements

Throughout the birthing of this novel, I have been blessed by much encouragement and support.

Unimaginable thanks to my entire family, especially to my daughters Kim and Stacey, and to my husband Bob Hallett; without their gifts of love and understanding this novel could not have been written. To Claire Verner, whose undying friendship and inconceivable strength have been my inspiration, I give my admiration and love.

Special thanks to The Faculty of Humanities and The Department of English for editorial (*dANDelion*) funding, to the English Department for graduate funding, including the A.T.J. Cairns Scholarship, and to Alberta Learning for an Alberta Heritage Award.

Finally, my thanks to Aritha van Herk. That she shares her knowledge and skill with her students is my great fortune. It has been an honor to work with and learn from the matriarch of contemporary Alberta fiction.

This book is dedicated to James Verner.

Table of Contents

PREFACE

"Altar Ego" is a novel which uses Calgary and its surrounding landscapes as the setting for a story about a mother and a daughter irrevocably coupled by rituals that connect marriage and death. Throughout the novel, marriage is a frame within which I have chosen to examine these characters, although neither is married at the time the story takes place. My novel, like those written by Charlotte Brontë and Jane Austen, takes up aspects of gender and property in the context of marriage. However, "Altar Ego" does not offer its female characters redemption and resolution as Brontë and Austen do in *Jane Eyre* and in *Sense and Sensibility*. Instead, convergence and confluence are characteristic of my novel, and aspects of marriage, gender, and property collide, causing indeterminable results for the characters.

"Altar Ego" began as a result of my interest in women's history and in the historical novel. The nineteenth century novel, specifically *Jane Eyre,* is important to my work, particularly in its treatment of marriage. When I read Brontë's narrative, I was struck by the story and by its fabula (Bal in *Narratology* 5). The novel presents a prescription for marriage that transitions the heroine from orphan to governess to wife. Brontë characterizes Jane / woman as a base unit of exchange whose movement within a complex social structure relies on gender and property.

In *Sense and Sensibility,* Jane Austen's Dashwood sisters actively seek the "office" of bride, imagining that it will help them to escape the restrictions of family life. In both Brontë and Austen the characters move from place to place. Jane Eyre progresses from governess to wife and the Dashwoods are rescued by marriage from their lot as property-bereft daughters. While my novel attempts to mirror the movement that Brontë and Austen's characters make, "Altar Ego" focuses on the behaviour of contemporary female characters outside of the model of marriage. My protagonist, Marlo Gilman, is a single woman who has moved to life outside wifedom numerous times. However, she still engages with aspects of her past marriages and is restricted in the present by her relationship with her mother, Bertha.

My novel is also influenced by historical accounts of early authors such as Julian of Norwich and Margery Kempe, who negotiated personal place / space in relation to marriage. Julian dedicated herself to religion instead of committing to marriage and to remaining the property of man. In her now famous *A Book of Showings,* Julian claims that her association with God informs her life and her words. Margery Kempe aligned her body with God and convinced her husband that she should live a life of celibacy after surviving "nearly twenty years of marriage and fourteen children" (Gilbert & Gubar 18). *The Book of Margery Kempe* rationalizes her relationship with God. Kempe began writing "when she was twenty-one, pregnant and in the midst of a disabling spiritual struggle, which she placed in the context of her visions of Christ on the one hand and her marital responsibilities on the other" (Gilbert & Gubar 19). What influences my work most in terms of Julian of Norwich and Margery Kempe is the power these women had to negotiate their place / space. By aligning themselves with God and religion they were able to resist the social and conjugal constraints of marriage. In "Altar Ego," Marlo forms an enduring attachment to property rather than aligning herself with the religion that defines her parents' beliefs. For Marlo, property is a non-negotiable possession that gives her financial power and that ultimately separates her from her father. Throughout my novel, she remains a sole proprietor of land, empowered at an early age by her recognition of the importance of self-agency.

I realize that many other instances of women and their relationships to marriage follow the historical examples I've given and that many other examples of marriage partnerships exist in literature. However, the nineteenth century novels I have used in my earlier examples best illustrate the origin of my interest in women and property and my interest in women *as* property in marriage.

In "Altar Ego" I have written about a mother and a daughter who are connected to each other and to marriage in typical familial ways, but I hope they can also be understood in relation to the marital details their story excludes. Bertha and Marlo Gilman are mercurial, slippery and difficult to grasp, characters who are limited and at the same time illimitable.

In *The Laugh of the Medusa*, Cixous speaks theoretically about women and women's writing. She says,

There is, at this time, no general woman, no one typical woman. What they have *in common* I will say. But what strikes me is the infinite richness of their individual constitutions: you can't talk about *a* female sexuality, uniform, homogenous, classifiable into codes—any more than you can talk about one unconscious resembling another. Women's imaginary is inexhaustible, like music, painting, writing: their stream of phantasm is incredible. (876)

By suggesting that women cannot be essentialized, Cixous' work implies that conditions exist for representing female characters outside prescribed social structures such as those represented in the nineteenth century novel. In "Altar Ego" I tried to represent female characters by focusing on their roles and actions outside marriage. These characters are not fixed by "*a*" prescribed connection to marriage, enclosed by gender, or limited by their relationship to property. My novel attempts to draw female characters whose lives converge with marriage, rather than characters like Jane Eyre who are defined by promises of social redemption in marriage.

Irigaray also takes up ideas of "infinite" woman in *Speculum*, specifically in her chapter entitled "Volume-Fluidity":

Woman is neither open nor closed. She is indefinite, in-finite, *form is never complete in her*. She is not infinite but neither is she *a* unit(y), such as a letter, number, figure in a series, proper noun, unique object (in a) world of the senses, simple ideality in an intelligible whole, entity of a foundation etc. This incompleteness in her form, her morphology, allows her continually to become something else, though this is not to say that she is ever univocally nothing. No metaphor completes her. Never is she this, then that, this and that. . . But she is becoming that expansion that she neither is nor will be at any moment as definable universe. (229)

Irigaray's ideas of "morphology" and of woman "continually becoming something else" suggest potential for representation. Her work infers that female characters can be represented in fiction as continually evolving persons.

In "Altar Ego," the Bow River is a metaphor for the limited and the illimitable, the definable and the indefinable, the ever-evolving and the indeterminable. In a localized sense, the river's physical conditions affect and support the characters in my novel. In terms of setting, an aquifer that progressively floods Marlo's property and a whirlpool at the base of Bertha's yard become underlying sources for journey, change, and growth. The water encroaching on both women's properties parallels the rising tension between them after the death of Ed, their father and husband. When they complete the first leg of their journey on the Bow they are more at ease with each other than they were before their excursion. Reciprocally, the water on Marlo's property is subsiding when they return to Calgary.

In terms of narrative framing, the flooding and the whirlpool also represent the degree to which both characters are connected to marriage, Marlo by a deluge of husbands and Bertha by the vortex of her solitary relationship to Ed. While I have characterized Marlo as someone who easily accepts change and who is eager to move on, Bertha is represented as a generational contrast. She is a woman enveloped by a tradition she dislikes, yet a woman unable to reject or travel past that tradition.

Motivation for the journey on the Bow River originates in the connection Marlo makes between her flooded property (166) and Ed's ashes, which Bertha hides in her garage (63). Marlo's suggestion that she and her mother canoe the river is also tied to her family's long-time connection with water. Her paternal grandparents have property on the north coast of Scotland, then settle in Calgary near the Bow River. Her grandfather reads on its banks after her grandmother dies (213). Bertha and Ed take over and build on the same land. Marlo buys the property and adds to the existing home when they decide to move downstream to a condominium (39).

Their collective history, which is rooted in settlement, can also be connected to representations of characters in a regional sense, especially in the context of travel, movement, and exploration of self. Connections between location and character are common in fiction. In a western Canadian context, in *Making it Home,* Deborah Keahey suggests that "the fact that so many selves have placed themselves in motion, moving from one place to another, raises the question of whether it is possible to go one step further and 'place' the self in motion, *while* in motion" (126). I hope that the characters in "Altar Ego" demonstrate that it is possible to represent the kind of movement or progression Keahey suggests. While physically traveling two segments of the Bow River (Lake Louise to Banff and Calgary to Carseland) Marlo engages introspectively with both narratives connected to marriage and with her associations to property. Marlo's past self converges with her present self whether she thinks about her wedding in Assiniboine Lodge (183), or the prospect of Joel in their former home (231). In writing these sections and others in the present tense, I have attempted to accomplish not only a sense of narrative movement between the past and the present but also to achieve a sense of immediacy for the reader.

Past and present also converge in the series of rhetorical questions Marlo asks throughout my novel. Her explorations of birth and death are grounded in the present but relate to her past pregnancy and abortion, and to her relationship with her father. When she is pregnant and travelling with her mother, she ponders the depth of maternal associations:

> How is silence constructed in the womb? Is it ever really quiet?
> Constant transference from mother to child via cable connection. An Intranet exclusively for two. Watery exchange, changing amniotic fluid, digestion, respiration, heart pumping, blood beating, lymph cleansing, kidneys processing, bowels bulging, host-mother voiding and avoiding.
> (41)

When her father dies, she ponders degrees of emotional disassociation from him by using a physical analogy similar to the one she uses to understand maternity:

> Do you ever wonder about death? Think about what the dying know that we don't? Wonder how many levels of consciousness are accessed in the process? . . . .I lie down next to Ed and place my hand on his chest. I wait—no resonance or renunciation from the vocal chords next to my ear. Digestion and respiration arrested. Blood and lymph immobilized. Bladder and bowel toothless. No more voiding or avoiding. (51-52)

9

For Marlo, the two events irrevocably link physical progressions involved in birth (growth) and death (decay).

In "Altar Ego," the female characters are represented and "constructed by movement" (Keahey 126) and by journey. Marlo is also characterized by the union of location, physical action, and emotion that converge during explorations such as the one she indulges in as she paddles across Lac Des Arcs:

> My grandfather read romance novels when he was eighty-eight. Poured over them with an intensity I'd never seen before. He took the old teak and canvas deck chairs down to the riverbank, set them up side by side and didn't come in until the book was done. Read one a day every day of the week except Sunday, the empty chair always next to him. (213)

In the previously cited paragraph and the next she also examines degrees of connection between married couples:

> Have you ever wondered at the depth of connection people have to each other? Sometimes I look at Bertha and I think that she's free of Ed and then I find her smelling his clothes or wearing his huge watch on her tiny wrist. (213)

She also comes to realize the strength and pull of her relationship with Bertha: "Whether she responds to me or not, she has the power to punctuate the conversation, speak in tongues, hold me at wordpoint" (245). Marlo ponders the characteristics that bind them, her rhetoric tied to the physical processes that connect them both to motherhood:

> Is the process of heredity involuntary? Or is the body of the mother in control of the process, like the one the egg uses to draw the millions of already dying sperm toward her? After she manages ejaculation and fertilization, does the mother send physical nourishment through the umbilical chord? Or does the embryo take what she needs? (245)

When Bertha can't quite master the j-stroke which steers their canoe (248) Marlo doesn't resist the impulse to continue an exploration of the change in their relationship to each other: "I wonder how it feels when you defer to your daughter. Maybe it's like separating the yolk from the egg using only your fingers" (249). While these two women live outside the confines of marriage and although they are characters "in motion, *while* in motion" (Keahey 126) they are never quite able to move past or resist the influences of family or its associated connections.

Marlo's thoughts culminate in a premonition that alludes to a drowning: "I dream that my mother and I cliff-jump; imagine the white of her legs and the red of her suit above me as I sink. I hold my breath, wake after my lungs fill with water, flailing and coughing" (259). In the section that follows Marlo's dream, the narrative foreshadows the physical separation of mother and daughter, who have in some respects been more engaged with each other than with their previous husbands. In this case Bertha is the partner who leaves, making preparations while they complete the last leg of their journey. "Bertha prays. Wraps the rosary around her wrist...picks up the crucifix. I watch as she touches the cross to her ears...touches [it to] the end of her nose" (260). Marlo is the partner who is not consciously aware of signs that indicate an ending. Bertha's gestures, which begin when she buries the "last" of Ed's ashes (248), mirror those included in the Catholic ritual of the Last Rites.

Marlo and Bertha's lives are connected geographically by the locations of their homes on the river, by continual movement, and by a stream of interruptions illustrated by the physical presence of each in the other's home and life. They are also "married" by their connections to motherhood and death. As Bertha supports her daughter's choice to abort a child (40-49), Marlo must come to understand her mother's decision to take her own life (265). Both women perform conscious acts of self-assured proprietorship. However, in what can be read as an allusion to an ultimate marital goal that Marlo never achieves with any of her husbands, she never imagines separating from Bertha.

The interaction of these two women throughout "Altar Ego" is supported by the Bow River and framed by the confluence of their connections with marriage, birth, and death. My novel ends with the suicide of Bertha Gilman. An initial reading of this event should provoke questions about the repetition of a nineteenth century trope where "general woman" (Cixous 876) cannot live without what I'll call for illustrative purposes "general man." The suicide asks the reader to consider the possibility of a narrative that confounds historical representations of female characters who take their own lives. Instead of writing this event as a "way out" for a woman who thinks she has no other option, I hope that Bertha's suicide can be read as an example of a self-conscious decision, an allusion to and a subversion of the figure of Bertha Rochester in *Jane Eyre*. My narrative attempts to advance the idea that Bertha Gilman, like her daughter, is a sole proprietor who purposely chooses when she will divest herself of her most prized property, that is herself.

Within the frame of marriage in "Altar Ego," proprietorship is a vital form of connection between mother and daughter. It also symbolizes the way in which I hoped that my narrative would write against historical examples of prescribed marriage, examples in which gender and property were irreconcilable. However, by using a marital frame "Altar Ego" also risks the re-affirmation of women and their relationship to marriage and property as they have been portrayed historically. In employing marriage as an irreconcilable sub-plot my novel tempts a reading of a contemporary social structure that still relies on gender and property, rather than solely provoking an examination of characters who are developed outside marriage.

By the end of my novel it is clear that marriage frames Bertha and Marlo, converges with their memories, and intrudes on their journey on the Bow River. What I hope is emphasized in "Altar Ego" is the narrative assertion that neither woman looks for nor expects redemption within that frame. Instead, and most importantly, both realize that the form of proprietorship which strengthens and irrevocably connects them is agency of self.

REFERENCES

Austen, Jane. <u>Sense and Sensibility</u>. Ed. Claudia L. Johnston. New York: Norton, 2002.

Bal, Mieke. <u>Double Exposures: The Subject of Cultural Analysis</u>. New York: Routledge, 1996.

---. <u>Narratology: Introduction to the Theory of Narrative</u>. Trans. Christine van Boheemen. Toronto: University of Toronto Press, 1997.

Bronte, Charlotte. <u>Jane Eyre</u>. Ed. Q.D Leavis. Harmondsworth: Penguin Books, 1979.

Cixous Helene. "Laugh of the Medusa." <u>Signs</u> 1.4 (1976): 875-893.

Gilbert, Sandra M. and Gubar, Susan, Eds. <u>The Norton Anthology of Literature By Women</u>. New York: W. W. Norton & Company, 1985.

Irigaray, Luce. "Volume-Fluidity." <u>Speculum of the Other Woman</u>. Ithaca, New York: Cornell University Press, 1985.

Keahey, Deborah. <u>Making it Home</u>. Winnipeg: University of Manitoba Press, 1998.

Showalter, Elaine. <u>The New Feminist Criticism: Essays on Women, Literature and Theory</u>. New York: Pantheon, 1985.

When text becomes context, when it leaves behind the single-minded project of following a singular life-line, when it drops out of narrative as climax and opts for narrative as interaction with what surrounds us, then we are in the presence...of a writing that ditches dualistic polarities...dodges the hierarchies...it's all there in the so-called 'nothing.'

Daphne Marlatt, "Self-Representation and Fictionalysis"

PROLOGUE

I've been interested in property all my life. I wondered who owned the womb I grew in. Wondered at five years of age why Bertha and Ed called me *their* child. Wondered at fourteen why they thought I was a commodity they would eventually trade.

I exchange houses for money and money for houses. I trade real estate, but I'm not the sort whose photograph appears in the weekend paper. I operate a private exchange for owners of waterfront properties on the Bow River. I am licensed to trade from Banff National Park to the place one hundred miles west of Medicine Hat where the Bow comes together with the Oldman River to shape the South Saskatchewan. These lands are my territory.

The properties I've traded include houses, an apartment building, a nursing home, condominiums, a restaurant, schools, single-family dwellings, farms, ranches, cottages, and cabins. I've concocted arrangements and ministered betrothals between Bow Terra Firma and people from around the globe, local millionaires, newlyweds, and couples of all genders. I've even followed through on the registration of land to a horse. Giddy-up.

I've married five men and I'm still not forty. That averages close to four years with each during my adult life, but the law of averages doesn't apply to marriage. Bertha and Ed stayed married for forty-three years. I stayed married to my second husband for less than seven days.

Five days ago my mother committed suicide by throwing herself in the Carseland weir. Four days ago her body and the remnants of my yellow Kevlar canoe surfaced near a bend in the Bow River on the Blackfoot Reserve. I had to ask permission from the band council to retrieve them. Three days ago my mother's bruised and bloated body was cremated. Yesterday I married my mother and father: ashes to ashes, dust to dust. *Bone of my bone,* she called him. Today I meet with Joel, my former second husband, to deliver a sealed message, the only other proprietary task my mother's will requires me to complete.

17

How I arrived at this particular conjuncture of life is not a puzzle. My story is not a mystery or a biography. My story is not even poetic; it is simply what happened in the space I inhabit.

Chapter I

The first thing Joel notices when he comes out west is the noise: thunderous and wet. Freezing rain pours ice on the aluminum lid of his tent trailer.

"Sounds like a tin basher with a ball peen hammer," he tells me.

I imagine an open origami. That night a bear paws him through the canvas, marks the tent with rancid pee, and rips the lids off his two coolers.

"Banana bread, raw eggs, cheese, marmalade, uncooked bacon, a pitcher of orange Tang, two gel freezer packs and a whole black pudding—completely consumed."

I'm the only one who believes his bear story.

"What's more frightening," he says, "is the wind."

Joel travels west and stops in Yoho National Park. After the bear rambles away he decides that his van is safer. Tells me that he bolts to the back doors, unlocks them, and then has to run back to the tent trailer for his sleeping bag. Locks the doors against the elements and sleeps on the corrugated floor until I wake him.

The noises emanating from the tent trailer startle Joel. He strains, hears the sound of trees leaning, wipes the van window with the forearm of his sweatshirt, and checks the blurred image for bears. He rolls over and opens the van doors. Looks out from the back. The plastic tablecloth that he fastened to the picnic table with v-shaped clips is half in the fire pit, half on the sodden ground.

I stare through a plastic window at the puddles that weigh the cloth down, let the canvas drop, let myself flop back on the trailer bed.

He shouts. Guttural sounds stick in his dry morning throat. "Get out! Get out of there! Yah—yah!" he yells. Claps as if slap-running a horse.

I wave a red shirt through the open trailer door.

He scrambles to his feet, runs the short distance from the van, and stops in front of me.

"Marlo Gillman," I say, extending my hand. I wear a pair of his thick wool socks, stare at the declining peak in his shorts.

His eyes search the trailer behind me.

"I was biking when the storm blew in," I continue, dropping my arm. "You're the only cover for miles, except for the campground caretaker, and he's a known asshole. Not many people out here in October."

Joel's bare feet leave the cold black dirt. I stand to the side. He circles behind me and stands arms out between the two wing-like beds. He leans his six-feet three-inch frame on the edge of a green sink, smirks at me as if I'm a regular guest.

"My bike is tucked under that end," I say, pointing.

"I didn't notice it outside," he says. The bed is strewn with my helmet and still damp clothes.

"My bike has a fourteen inch frame," I say.

"Those are *my* jacket and socks."

"Sorry. I was soaked. Look, I'll get dressed and be on my way."

"Joel," he says. He thrusts his hand forward, "Richards." He loosens his grip, smooths his hands down the front of his shorts, holds them there one over the other.

"I apologize—I—"

"I'm used to neighbors turning up at our place when I come in after checking the cattle, but not strange women wearing my socks." He looks at my legs.

"I live in Calgary," I say. "I was riding back from Takakkaw Falls after visiting a friend who works in Whiskey Creek Hostel. The wind I can deal with. The freezing rain—made me take cover, too treacherous to peddle for Banff. Where are you from?"

"Cypress Hills—originally."

"Alberta or Saskatchewan?"

"Saskatchewan," he says. "Quiet and dry."

I smile then, think he's okay.

"I should be angry!" he says, voice rising. "This isn't an alpine hut!"

"Listen, I'll put on my gear and ride out." I pick up my belongings.

He scratches his head. His ponytail twitches above his shoulder blades. I feel his eyes on my skin four inches above my knees where my freckles stop.

"That fridge behind me has a pack of coffee, a carton of cigarettes, and a loaf of bread in it," he says, pointing.

"That's a fridge?" I look at the faded avocado door.

"Yeah. Works off the propane bottle. Listen, let me offer you something before you go."

"I don't smoke."

"Coffee then?"

"I quit drinking that stuff when I turned thirty."

"Toast?"

"I'm allergic to yeast."

"Look, it's all I have. Bear took off with my coolers last night."

"Never camped before?" I clutch the thin bundle of clothes to my chest, squeeze past him through the doorway.

"Wait! I have cans of stuff—cereal—crackers—under there." He points to a wooden box that doubles as a seat.

I flip my long red braid over my shoulder.

"My family runs an outfitter's cabin on the Highwood."

"Thought you were from Cypress Hills?"

"Now we ranch between Longview and Kananaskis."

"Do you have any toothpaste?"

"Toothpaste?"

"Bears love it. Will do almost anything to get it. Toothpaste and discarded tampons." It's my turn to make him nervous. "I do apologize. I thought the van was empty. I looked in last night and couldn't see anyone—didn't see you. I called *Hello*, a few times, then I came in here—"

"My folks will shit when I tell them the trailer stayed up in the wind."

"What?"

"Almost crushed my sister last year. Someone forgot to lock the crank."

"I think I'll get dressed," I say, pointing to the outhouse.

I retrieve my bike shoes from under the trailer and walk on my toes to the small log building four campsites away. When I come back he's humming Dvorak. I feel underdressed in my padded cycling shorts and fitted neoprene shirt. I knock on the metal body of the ancient trailer. The coffee aroma is uninviting, but I accept the hot mug when Joel offers it. Let it brand my palms red.

≈≈≈

I'm reading about a property in Inglewood three weeks later when Joel calls about his socks.

"Who was that?" Bertha asks, after she eavesdrops for forty minutes.

"Just someone I met when I visited Nemit at Whiskey Creek."

"Nemit?" She looks at me over the frame of her reading glasses. "The caller is female?"

"Male," I say.

"Pretty long conversation."

"Pretty long."

"What's going on?"

"I'm thinking about using some of my inheritance from Gran to invest in a house."

Bertha hates that I don't answer her questions. Declares that she loves me when I introduce her to the tall, dark sock-owner a month later. Is horrified when we tell her the story of how we met. Is disappointed five years later when I tell her we won't be married in a church.

≈≈≈

"Joel and I have decided." I wear a track in the basement Berber.

"Decided?" Bertha says.

"Decided," I say, taking in the view of the Bow river from the walkout basement in Bertha and Ed's semi-detached bungalow.

"Decided what?"

"To hold a ceremony," I say. My eyes are drawn to the pool the river makes at the bottom of their property in the spring.

"A w-wedding ceremony?"

"A wedding ceremony."

"Yes! I knew you'd come to your senses! I'll call Auntie and let her know, and she can call Reed and his girlfriend, and of course we'll have to have your Dad's family over from the old country. You'll have to let some of them stay at the old house. His brother and wife have—"

"Six kids," I say, turning. "They're not invited."

"Not invited?" Bertha jerks her body off the flowered couch.

"Not invited. The location we've chosen isn't very accessible."

"Not accessible?"

"We want to get married at Mount Assiniboine Lodge."

"In the mountains?" The color on her face deepens and she paces through the room.

"Ed!" I call from the bottom of the stairs. "Can you please get Mum to stop repeating everything I say?"

"No," he says, making his way down.

"Eddie! Don't you dare!" Bertha says.

"Girls!" his tongue vibrates the hard r. "All right you two—I'll brew the tea. Bertha, sit yourself down—and you, missy Marlo, give your mother a chance. Would you please? If you canny do that, then I just don't know."

"I'll need more than a cup of tea to settle me!" Bertha says.

"Okay, just a wee minute then. Marlo, will you have a dram as well?" His index finger and thumb waggle back and forth.

I sit across from Bertha in Ed's wingback chair, wait for his squat body to climb the stairs. "Thanks."

"Breathe in, breathe out," Bertha mutters.

"We just want to keep it simple." My feet hang off the footstool.

"Simple!"

"Bertha."

"Marlo! How do you expect people—expect us to get in there?" She can't stay still. "I'm not hiking for two days, fighting off bears, or sleeping in a tent to watch you get married in a pair of hiking boots!" She re-traces the track I made in front of the door.

"Calm yourself, lovey—here's your drink."

"Thanks Ed," Bertha says to him.

He hands me a tumbler and downs his own. Wipes the back of his hand across his mouth. "An' you," he says, pointing, "call me *Dad* or I'll not be riding in any helicopter."

"Helicopter?"

"Helicopter, Bertha," I say.

"Jesus, Mary, and Joseph," she says, crossing herself. "Okay, I won't say another word until I get the whole story."

"Okay," I say.

"Okay," she repeats.

"September long weekend. We've booked the lodge. You two, Auntie and Reed, Joel's mum and his sister chopper in the Friday afternoon. I'll send some things with you, the cake and my dress and Joel's clothes. The—JP will fly in Saturday."

"A J fucking P?" Ed spits.

"You promised to wait until I was done."

"A Justice of the fucking Peace."

"You promised."

"I did no such thing. That was your mother. I'll have no part in a wedding that's not recognized by the Church." The tumbler waves about in his left hand.

"Ed!" Bertha takes the glass from him. "My Edinburgh crystal."

"I'm your f—ing Dad, and by God this time I'm on your mother's side!"

"Ed, sit down," Bertha says.

"I'm willing to hold my tongue for a lot a' things, but you know how I feel about heathen weddings. It's a bloody sin not to be joined in holy wedlock by a priest who is—"

"God's agent on earth. Yes dear," Bertha says. "Breathe in, breathe out."

"Maybe I should come back when you've had time to digest the idea," I say, standing.

"Digest the I-dear?"

"You're doing what she does!" I say.

"She!—That's your mother and don't you bloody well forget it young lady!"

"Daddy, please."

"Och, don't. You know I canny stand it when you call me that."

"Eddie, let's give her a chance to explain," Bertha interrupts.

"Bloody hell—at least tell me it's a man."

"It's a woman."

"I'm going to the shop!" Ed leaves through the sliding door. I watch him grab the old Triang bike and push it across the lawn.

"He'll catch his overalls in the chain."

"I know," Bertha says. "Just give him a while, okay? You've made a choice and we'll respect it the best we can—without *liking* it, mind."

"Don't like my groom?"

"Don't be daft."

"It's a beautiful place—"

"Next to what? You know we go to the cathedral once a month and Saint Bernard's every other Sunday for mass. You can marry in either Church if you like."

"Think of Assiniboine as another one of God's places."

"I don't think there's a throne for any bishops up there."

"Bertha, it is beautiful. You love our slides. The mountain is as grand as the Matterhorn."

"I'd rather go to Italy. Strike that. Switzerland."

"I'm wearing a dress."

"A dress?"

"A wedding dress."

"A wedding dress?"

"Yes."

"What about the flowers? Let us at least get those. Please?"

"Okay."

"And Ed, he'll want to pay for the meal—and the liquor. Have you been shopping? What do you think you want to wear? Long? Short? Mid-length? A veil? A headdress? I still have the hat I wore. A hat with a veil! Those are really popular right now."

"Bertha—I've—"

"What about the menu? Tell me we're not eating three courses of healthy vegetarian? Ed will expect meat and potatoes."

"We're not eating three courses of vegetarian. There's a full service kitchen. The lodge will house our family and a group from Spain."

"Spaniards. Good God, Ed won't like that!"

"What?"

"I'll need a mother of the bride outfit. A coat dress—with a hat!"

≈≈≈

And so it went with Bertha. She was always animated. The fishermen standing on the riverbank the day she died swore she was wearing a hat. *Blue pillbox*, one of them said. *Just like the kind Jackie O used to wear, net over the eyes. Held onto it as she went under.*

And Ed. Ed was loud, ideas chiseled in sacred stone, until you let him bevel the edge. For that maneuver, I needed Joel, knew that man-to-man was the only way that Ed would concede.

≈≈≈

"Hi Ed."

"Jo—el."

"Better be careful."

"I like pacing on this beam. It's the first piece of equipment I ever got for Marlo. Got it when the Mount Royal Gym Club was upgrading."

Ed glares at Joel. Transfers his weight from one foot to the other. Joel sits on the workbench next to Ed's toolbox and listens.

"Listen son," Ed continues, "I know that we all like to please our women, but I just canny imagine you not getting married in a Church."

"I'm okay with that."

Ed executes a slow spin on the ball of his left foot, plants the right in front. "You're okay wi' that? Well that's just grand. Insult to injury man. Insult to injury."

I used to practice on that beam every day. Ed put the four-inch wide wood in the middle of the lawn and watched me prance, cartwheel, and break my ankle trying to land my back somersault.

"We'll still be legal."

"No' in the eyes of God."

"You're upset because the JP is a woman."

Managing Ed's reactions was always a delicate balancing act, an act that Bertha perfected, a performance that ran until Ed died. Joel and I were supporting actors.

"Good God man. Where's your sense of integrity? The Pope doesn't see fit to put women in the priesthood. Far too emotional. So what does this thing you're doing say aboot that?"

"It says we're progressive."

"Progressive my arse. I might as well just bend over an' let you give me the what for."

"Things are different now, Ed."

"I didn't raise her to be sacrilegious."

"She respects your dedication to the Church."

"Ma' Church? Ma' bloody Church?"

Ed steps off the beam and circles a pool of sawdust in the middle of the shop floor.

"We hope you can find your way to respect our—choices."

"That's the trouble with you lot, too many bloody choices. That's why the Catholic Church is successful world-wide—it preaches restraint."

"It preaches guilt."

"Careful boy-o."

"The Church doesn't allow people to make their own choices."

"You're stepping over a line!"

"Ed listen, you and Bertha had one child. You can't tell me you didn't use some method of birth control—"

"Bertha's and my sex life is none of your concern. What the hell has that daughter of mine done to you? She's poisoned your mind wi' her female burn the bra crap."

"She'd laugh at you for that."

"Aye, she would."

Ed lifts the hood of the Rover, checks the oil.

"Took me a long time to figure out what you were talking about," Joel says.

"And now?" Ed asks, pulling the long stick out of its casing.

"And now I think I understand her—"

"Your first mistake, son!" He cleans the oil off the end. "She locked me in here once," he says, replacing the wavering length of metal.

"What?"

Ed backs away from the car and Joel pulls the dipstick.

"Aye, she did that. Paid for it dearly as well. Did she not tell you? Oil looks fine."

"No," Joel laughs.

"It was no laughing matter. I refused to let her miss mass when she was ten. She wanted to go to Brownie camp. I helped her get ready, even helped her design a kite frame so she could get a badge for something or other. Then I found out she'd be away all day and night on a Sunday, so I said no. Said she'd be cast out by the Lord, that she'd burn up in the fires o' hell. So she locked me in the shop. I didn't know until I tried to go in for supper two hours later. Before Marlo turned the shop into a garage, mind, all we had was the side door. Had a padlock on the outside. She went in, told her mother that I was lacquering and that I'd be a while. So the two of them go over to Jane's to get away from the smell. There I was screaming like a banshee when Bertha came back."

"And Marlo?" Joel asks him.

"The conniving wee bugger stayed the night with her cousin, Reed. The whole point is—I missed the Wednesday night Knights of Columbus mass—"

"Shite!"

"Right you are there boy-o! Bertha left her at Jane's for the rest of the week. When she came home she wasn't the least bit sorry. So I made her miss her Brownies on the following Monday and made her write lines for two and a half hours."

"Lines?"

"In school, if we'd done something bad, we had tae write, *I will not*—whatever it was, hundreds of times in our best printing—in addition to a pelting with the strap."

Joel said he was a bit concerned at that point. Never pictured Ed as that kind of a father. He must have had a strange look on his face because Ed went on, "Now wait a wee minute—I never hit that lassie! No indeed. But she did have to write, *I will not lock Ed in the shop*, the whole time she should have been in her Pixie group. She was the sixer."

"Did she do it?"

"Aye. And at the end was a wee prayer that thanked God for sparing her Daddy from the burning fires o' hell."

≈≈≈

And so it went with Ed.

"You were a bad kid," Joel tells me later.

"He did miss mass and survive," I say.

I had a point to make with Ed when I was ten. Joel made my point again later by not making a point about the wedding. He let Ed carve out his own angle. I was more to the point with Ed when I was a kid, now I'm soft, more like Bertha. Except when it comes to property.

Ed never believed that I could manage or exchange land, waited daily for me to get into financial trouble. Love-hated my determination. I disgraced him when I divorced Domenic and dishonored him when I married Joel outside the Church. He didn't understand what was important to me. I didn't buy into the shame the Church preached or the guilt he worshipped. But he came to the wedding. The last one he attended. He made one request—that he read a blessing from the Catholic wedding liturgy. I conceded.

≈≈≈

When they arrive at the Shark Mountain pick-up point, the chopper is already on the ground. It's thirty-five minutes after the appointed meeting time. The wait costs me the price of another ticket, one hundred and twenty-five dollars.

"Thought you weren't going to show," the pilot says.

"One word," Ed replies.

"Women?" the pilot asks.

"Drunks."

Jane gets out of the car and scowls at Ed. Reed throws up the remnants of the previous night's revelry. Ed stomps about, loads four boxes of wedding paraphernalia into the back of the chopper.

"You should've seen what he did with the cake!" Bertha tells me later.

She and Jane carry small overnight bags that they stow under the seats and then Bertha makes one last trip to the car for the dress. She holds it at arm's length, watches the garment bag twist hideously in the wind before Jane helps to fold the dress neatly over her arm.

"As though the dress was trying to get away!" Jane says that night.

They are still on the ground forty-four minutes later.

"It's a wedding," Jane says, her voice low and soothing. "Could you possibly make an exception? I'm sure he's fine now."

"He ought to be," Ed says. "He spewed all over the side of ma car—look at it! What's that going to be like after two days in the September sun?"

"Nothing left," Reed says. "I'm sure of it."

"Against my better judgment," the pilot finally says to Reed. "Okay—you—in the back, please," he points to Jane. "You too," he says, nodding at Ed. "Lady with the dress—in the front."

"I'm fine now—really," Reed laughs, wipes his mouth. "Nothing that some hair of the dog won't cure."

"Get in. Probably better than saddling the next group with you."

Reed climbs in the back next to his mother.

The pilot checks the gear and the harnesses, then gives Ed a headset. "You'll hear everything I say, but no talking until after take-off," he warns.

"The pilot *liked* Bertha," Ed tells me later.

"Getting married?" he asks Bertha.

"My daughter is," she laughs.

"Well, I've flown a few brides. Some dumb enough to fly in full regalia."

"Not Marlo."

"Same thing about the headset," he says to Bertha.

"Same thing, thanks."

The pilot presses his index finger to his lips and closes the door, checking the handle lock as he does. He climbs in the other side, flips a switch, turns a key and the rotor spins.

"Jesus, Mary, and Joseph," Bertha says into the mike.

The pilot smiles and points at a Saint Christopher medallion glued to the instrument panel.

"Patron saint of travel," comes from the back seat.

Bertha shrugs and smiles, turns and looks at Ed, puts her index finger to her lips. They cross themselves.

The revolutions increase. They listen to the base radio in Canmore. Bertha clutches the dress and the edge of her seat as the ground falls away and the car shrinks. She lets out a faint cry when the machine turns and rises.

I have to hang the dress in the lodge kitchen to steam out the wrinkles.

"There's a bit of a wind today but not enough to make too much of a difference to the flight," the pilot says, looking back at Ed. "And, we've had snow overnight."

Ed notices the two handed grip and the tension that makes every vein in the pilot's forehead and arms stand out.

"Lovely," Bertha says.

Ed is quiet. He listens to the sound of the wind over the blades. Jane's eyes are closed. Reed's head is between his knees.

The pilot grins. "Ever been up before?" he asks Bertha.

"No—Is it always the non-hiker types then?"

"Usually climbers who think the hike is too boring."

Bertha looks around. "We can't see the Bow Valley Corridor—what's that road though?"

"The Smith Dorian. Those," he adds after a few minutes, "are the Sunshine meadows." He gestures ahead with his chin.

"Most interesting passenger?"

"Rick Hansen."

"Rick Hansen?"

"Wheelchair athlete—travelled the world. Came up here for a month when he got back."

"Shite," says Ed. He grabs a bag and heaves.

"Should've known. It's always the quiet ones," the pilot says.

Reed laughs.

"There it is!" Bertha exclaims like a child. "Mount Assin-ay-boine."

"Don't think the group of climbers I flew in two days ago are going all the way. Look at the snow." The chopper nears the pass.

"This is fantastic!" Bertha cries.

The whup-whup reaches us before they skim the meadow. We watch them follow the creek. The space blanket I'm lying on flashes on the ground.

"Look! It's our kids!" Bertha shouts.

"Och, don't be daft," Ed replies, craning his neck.

"Lake Magog," the pilot says. "And the peak. It's usually shrouded in cloud."

Before the pilot grounds the machine on a wooden platform he circles above the lodge.

"It's not like a falling sensation," Bertha says later. "It's as if the ground breathes out."

I reach the pad ahead of Joel. I'm running as the chopper lifts off. Bertha waves madly, doesn't care about her mother of the bride hair-do. Ed, Jane, and Reed crouch behind an outhouse, holding the dress down.

"Mum! Dad!" I yell. I throw my arms around Ed and say, "There's a Bishop in the lodge!"

≈≈≈

Bishop to Rook, Knight to Queen, Queen takes Knight. Moves. We all make them. I make one that ends in checkmate—my partner foursquare against me.

I buy the house in Inglewood. I barter and the price is reduced to compensate for the ailing furnace, the plaster and lath walls, the ancient electrical, and the rusted five-gallon hot water tank, which was a luxury in its day. I buy the house and add it to my holding company.

Properties that my company managed then included the house I live in and the four apartments that I rent. I don't buy stock or mutuals. I don't register money for retirement. I invest in property. I began when my grandmother broke her husband's heart and sold the land near John O' Groats. Granny gifted me one thousand pounds. I split the money and bought two apartments. She co-signed, provided collateral when Ed wouldn't. I rented the apartments to a divorced couple in seventy-eight. The wife lived on the third floor. The husband lived in the basement. They each paid two hundred and fifty dollars a month. Ten years later, I'm the owner of twelve hundred square feet in a five story concrete building. I use one apartment as collateral, double down and buy two more.

Ed says I haven't an ounce of good sense, taking chances like that—without a man to back me up. *What happens,* he asks, *when the interest rates go up?* Worries about bailing me out when mortgages fly up to eighteen percent. I'm locked in at ten and a half.

Granny dies. Ed tears at his hair when I offer him cash for the old house. Bertha smiles through her tears. I tell him he can use the shop whenever he wants for as long as he's able. He drops the price and shakes my hand. My parents move to an adult complex one kilometre downstream. Park the Rover in the new garage.

The Inglewood house doesn't have a garage. Ed rides his bike from Bowness the day I sign the papers. He wants to know why Joel isn't party to the deal. Wants to know what I think I can really own without my man. Wants to know if I hear what he says. I plan and arrange, marry Joel anyway.

Chapter II

Have you ever noticed how acute your hearing is during menstruation? I always want to scream, *Stop yelling at me!* but I know I'll only hurt myself. The river sends waves crashing through the skull. The kitchen clock emulates Big Ben and Joel's feet sound like nails on a blackboard when he crosses the tile floor.
This isn't really menstruation.

Through the umbilical cord—the noise—is it as loud? Is it magnified or muted by the surrounding viscosity? Surely the mother is heard, sensed. Foetal ears function in the womb.

What is the term for the sludge and clump-filled flow left over in a vacuumed and roughly vacated womb? Vacation. I tell him I am going on a little trip with Bertha—shopping.

"In Kalispell?" he asks, voice rising. "What can you possibly buy there?" He knows I sink every penny into my house. "Bertha makes you crazy."

"I have to go with her—I promised."

Joel thinks I'm still looking for a wedding dress.

I drive. As the city haze fades behind us I let her do the talking. She describes and embellishes. Rails about Ed, complains about Ed, and laughs about their latest trip together for one hour and twenty-two minutes, before she really looks at me.

"I brought money," she says. Then silence.

How is silence constructed in the womb? Is it ever really quiet? Constant transference from mother to child via cable connection. An intranet exclusively for two. Watery exchange, changing amniotic fluid, digestion, respiration, heart pumping, blood beating, lymph cleansing, kidneys processing, bowels bulging, host-mother voiding and avoiding. Virtual reality. Longview framed in the rear view.

Have you ever noticed how shrewd your mother is when she analyzes you? I always want to scream, *Stop staring at me!* but I know I'll only hurt myself. Her Joy fills my nostrils. The bananas she stores in the snack-pack make me nauseous and the smell of mothballs, which always takes a while to wear off her spring clothes, melts the windshield.

Joel insists on cleaning my car before I leave. Dusts the dashboard, washes the windows, caramelizes the chrome—no streaks, no spotting allowed.

"Do you want me to drive?" Bertha asks, when we reach the Frank Slide.

"Thanks," I say, pulling over. The idea of lives flattened and ripped and vacuum-sealed under the mounds of boulders is daunting. Is death quick? Is there a lot of blood? Low blood pressure and the move to standing after sitting for so long make me light-headed. I meet Bertha by the trunk.

"Breathe in, breathe out," I hear her mutter as she flutters her fingers over her abdomen, womb height. Her feet dance the same way mine do. I grab her hands and imagine we polka. She walks with me to the passenger door.

"Fine?" she asks, stroking my hair.

"Fine." I close my eyes and sink into the reclined seat so that I don't have to watch her squat-pee in the ditch.

Have you ever noticed how slack your mouth is when you sleep in a car? Towns never taste the same complemented by engine hum, and mother hum, and the burn of dried drool. Frank—cooked ham; Coleman—pickles and gherkins; Blairmore—roasted garlic and freshly turned vegetable gardens; Sparwood—Cajun egg-noodles.

The smell of the semi-red sauce smothering Bertha's lunch assaults me. I drink water. I order plain rice when Bertha finishes. She talks—talks about Auntie and my cousin Reed. I decide ahead of time not to balk at the ritual I know she'll insist on before we continue.

≈≈≈

I take pictures of her. She is a dwarf next to the incomprehensible rubber of the world's largest dump truck. She moves from black tire to lime green body, like Baggins beginning a quest. She stands under the front bumper.

"Boost me!" she demands. "Ed showed me a little trick the last time we stopped here."

"Bertha—"

"Bertha," she mimics.

I brace myself, one foot slightly behind the other, hands clasped at knee height. She steps onto them, one hand on my shoulder; she reaches up and unleashes a telescoping ladder. This is one of the few times in my life I am glad my mother is smaller than my sixty-one and three-quarter inches and lighter than my one hundred and eighteen pounds.

"Da, daa!" she sings, easing her weight from my shoulders.

She climbs onto the bumper, then she carefully makes the transition to the fixed ladder that scales the front of the Titan between the grill and the headlight. She poses on the first rung, Bilbo-ing her face at me. Says, "Come on! Let's climb this monster!"

I follow her up, and we stand on the fenced platform in front of the windshield. We stare through the windows at the huge box. She grabs my hand and raises it over our heads, heels lifting like a pumped up jogger. "Da, da, daa—da, da, daa. Na, na, naa—na, na, naa!" she sings, spreading out the syllables. "See honey," she says, "in the grand scheme of things how insignificant everything is?"

"Ma'am! Miss!" Neither of us noticed the white and crossbar lit car pulling into the parking lot next to the highway. "I'll have to write you up," the officer says. "Trespassing. Two hundred and fifty each."

"Five hundred bucks! Then son, we want a picture. Honey—give him the camera." She takes the small automatic from her fanny pack.

I drop it toward the officer wearing the single bee stripe on his legs. Bertha puts her scrawny arm around my shoulder and cradles my bent head on her bony breast. I stare at the enormous box past the pink of my mother's clothes and can't imagine her without me. The sign inside the back says, *Payload = 350 tons.*

≈≈≈

Have you ever noticed that blood doesn't evaporate? After we cross the border at Roosevelt the sides of the highway are lined with crosses. I imagine that the surface I'm driving on coagulates.

"That young officer is thick," Bertha interrupts.

"Thick?"

"Thick. He gave Ed and me a ticket for climbing the Titan. But the last time he saw me I had just completed a demo climb for Jane. She wouldn't go up."

"Wouldn't go up?"

"Wouldn't take the Titan challenge. She's far too prissy. Even when we were kids she had a holier-than-thou attitude. Walked as if she was wrapped in a straight jacket. Now she's stuck with that sap of a son who follows her everywhere, bleeds her for money every chance he gets."

Does the flow of blood from mother to child occur during each diastolic pause? The foetus engorging and gorging itself? I'm animated when I walk into the building in Kalispell, drained when Bertha helps me walk out. I want to scream, but I know I'll only hurt myself. I fall asleep as she drives north.

≈≈≈

I wake when the engine stops.

"We're in Whitefish," Bertha says softly, as I struggle to open my eyes. "Wait here. I'll check in." Her hand traces a line from my temple to my chin.

The drive from Kalispell doesn't exist. My eyes can't focus but I know the lake is behind the row of cabins.

"Number five," Bertha says, when she comes back with the key.

Have you ever noticed how compassionate your mother is when you're in pain? I want to yell, *Stop patronizing me*, but I know I'll only hurt myself. Bertha opens the passenger door and lets me take her arm. I'm barren and she's ripe. Inside the cabin she helps me lower my body onto a chaise in front of the huge windows. I think she covers me with a blanket.

I dream that when I lift my head my long hair stays behind, the thickness and length of my life cut away. I imagine picking up handfuls and holding them below my ears.

"Good morning Rapunzel!" a voice sings. I turn my head toward the sound. Think my right hand hurls strands. Feel tears streaming.

"Shshshshshshsh," a voice whispers.

I remember placing my feet on cold metal.

"Shshshshsh," Bertha croons.

I dream that a thumb crosses a switch, imagine that a flexible tube ripples.

"Marlo," my mother's voice whispers.

I feel her warm hand caressing my head, believe that there's hair in my still clenched fists. I raise my left hand to throw clumps on the floor. My breath comes in spasms.

I open my eyes and look out over the lake, see patches of ice on its surface. My eyelids droop. A rod jigs in my hand. I wind a metal handle. A fish swims away.

Have you ever noticed the beauty in the lines on your mother's face? They make me want to cry. I dream. Red silk skims bare feet, catches my mother's attention. When I awake Bertha helps me move across the black and white floor to the bedroom.

≈≈≈

"Knight to Queen." Bertha slides the piece across the chessboard.

"You can't take advantage of me like this," I say.

"Why not?"

"I'm weak."

"Not my fault if you didn't pay attention when Ed taught you how to play."

"Couldn't let him teach me how to drive either."

I take her Knight with my Rook. She advances her Bishop.

"Checkmate!" she says.

"All right! All right! I'm going for a walk."

"A walk?"

"A walk, Bertha. Out there," I say, pointing at the lake.

Have you ever noticed how devious your mother is when she plays games? I always want to laugh. I stay in the cabin for two days letting her nurse me. The temperature plummets soon after we check in. Today the man at the front desk calls to say that it's minus fifty at the top of the mountain, in case we are thinking about spring skiing, but there is no snow here.

"It's freezing," she says.

"Yes?"

"Sure you feel up to it?"

"Yes."

"Want me to come?"

"No."

I walk carefully down the long flight of wooden stairs that lead to the rocky beach. My quads shake and I wonder how they'll feel when I have to go up. I stop at the bottom—think I hear a flute. I decide to walk south toward the main road. I turn and wave up at Bertha who stands outside on the deck.

"Careful!" she calls.

"Yes Mummy!"

Have you ever noticed the noise that water makes when it breaks ice? Liquid laps the beach in tiny waves; the lake moves below its late skin, forces pure sound through blowholes. I pull my hat lower on my forehead. I lean against a huge log. I don't know how long I've been here when I detect a loud plop-hiss between notes. I lift my head and see a sheepskin-clad man about a hundred yards away. The coat is the same colour as his sandy hair. He wears roper style boots and syncopates the lake's rhythm. He raises his hand, waits for a note, throws.

"That's the Phillips boy." Bertha breaks the strange cadence.

Have you ever noticed how your mother can sneak up on you when you least expect her? I don't scream. I let her hug me.

"The Phillips *boy*?"

"The family came here every year at the same time we did for twelve years and you don't recognize him?"

"Don't know." I look at the man. Note the lined face.

"Well, he is a fair bit older than you," she whispers.

He reaches us a couple of minutes later.

"Mrs. Gillman! And?"

"Marlo," I say.

"Tho—mas!" A woman calls from the door of a cabin that spirals smoke into the air.

"My mother," he says. "Nice to see you both."

I watch him lope over the uneven ground. I see him again several years later in a lobby with Nemit. Marry him a few months after that.

Chapter III

Dust billows behind Nemit's vehicle on Dunbow Road, overtakes her car as she turns onto the shale driveway in front of the large house.

I'm showing a property just south of the city. "The potential is unlimited," I say. "The view of downtown is quite subtle, close enough to enthral your guests in the evening, far enough to let you enjoy the river."

I open the dining room window and let the couple savour the afternoon breeze.

"Expecting another buyer?" the man asks me. He looks upset. "We called you because you understand—no pressure, our colleagues said."

"None," I say. "The driver is a friend. I can't imagine why she's come here."

I wonder if Nemit has lost her job, if she's finally pregnant again, or if Joy has followed through on her threat to leave. Then I think about Joel. Maybe he's come back. "Excuse me," I say after I open the French doors to the glass-rimmed deck. I leave the couple looking across the sloping property that ends fifty feet above the Bow River and meet Nemit at the door.

"It's Ed," she manages. Her face is streaked with tears.

"Not Joel?"

"Your mother called me."

Bertha refuses to speak with Nemit. Pleasantries are all she can manage. "Bertha doesn't call you."

"You have to come."

"I'll be about another hour."

"Your Dad," she stutters.

"Ed?"

≈≈≈

"A heart attack," Bertha whispers between breaths into Ed's mouth when I finally arrive.

43

I enter the room and imagine Ed's voice, remember him talking about books with his father. I don't comfort Bertha, or go with her when she's taken from the room. For a moment I think I see Ed standing in the corner, but when I look too hard, he disappears. His body is prone on the bed.

I kneel and take his hand, curl his fingers in mine. "I'll stay," I tell the paramedic, remember what my Granny tells me about leaving.

Do you ever wonder about death? Think about what the dying know that we don't? Wonder how many levels of consciousness are accessed in the process? Do our perceptions change as our organs shut down? Do we adapt, as if sightless or deaf? Does the loss of our senses separate us from what we know? When we can't smell or taste or touch, do the organs take over? Liver and kidney, pancreas and spleen, lungs, heart and brain, does each provide a sensation? Let us recognize impulses that we only distinguish at emancipation? Force us to let go of anger and love? Is death like impotence?

I lie down next to Ed and place my hand on his chest. I wait—no resonance or renunciation from the vocal chords next to my ear. Digestion and respiration arrested. Blood and lymph immobilized. Bladder and bowel toothless. No more voiding or avoiding.

I listen to the story waft from the kitchen. Ed carries a box of ash. The man next door sees him fall. Calls nine-one-one. Neighbours bring Ed inside. Bertha starts CPR. People stare and cry.

I look for the gaze that holds me all my life, but the eyes are dull. The lids opened, pupils shrunken, retinas denying reflection. The image I thought I saw there did not survive, never existed. I hear a sigh.

Chapter IV

What I know of my mother's actions after Ed dies comes directly from her journal. I remember her account of events without conscious change, although alterations must occur because I picture her antics and then translate them. The events that took place before her death were both tangential and surreal.

≈≈≈

My mother kneels in front of the urn containing my father's ashes. Her small hands caress the sides of the metallic vessel.

"It's time for you to move on," she says. "Five feet four inches reduced to one hundred, eighteen and a half cubic inches. I must have been distraught when I chose cremation."

She lifts the blinds behind the Jacuzzi tub where the urn sits. The neighbors are on their patio having coffee. "Look at you; I couldn't get you out of your overalls unless there was sex involved, then I found this tub, remember? Sex. What a novel idea."

She backs away and sits on the toilet, elbows on her knees, hands under her chin. "I miss you, Ed. You're hardly in my dreams any more and you don't listen when I'm talking."

Her hands move to her thighs. "What happens at the six-month mark? God demands that you rise up? The angels come down and say, *Fly with us?* Peter gets impatient at the pearly gates? I don't feel you any more."

Her nails move across her red corduroy pants. She palms her breasts in a circular motion. The starched fabric of my father's best white shirt grazes her skin. "I'm getting you out of there," she says.

Her hands slap her thighs.

≈≈≈

"Bertha!" Betty and Stan call between sips. "How are you today, sweetie?"

"Bloody peachy."

"Cleaning out the fireplace trap then are we?"

"Yep."

"Stan, why don't you do that for her?"

"Here, let me help you, luv," Stan offers.

Bertha gets up from her squat in front of the chimney and walks quickly over the small green space between her home and her neighbors'.

"Oh, my. Oh, my," Betty ejects. Stan is motionless, Ed's white shirt transparent in the sun.

"Here ducks, you sit and I'll take care of that for you. Won't take me but a moment." Stan's singsong voice falters just enough to delight Bertha.

She stretches her arms up and rewards the man for staring. Gives him a peck on the cheek. "Thanks Stan," she says, before she sits in his chair and lifts his coffee cup.

"Wait luvey, let me get you a fresh one," Betty says, but Bertha has already taken a sip. "That warm enough for you? Would you like anything else? A doughnut? A bagel? A Bismarck?"

"No thank you, Betty."

"You're getting awfully thin, Bertha. Are you eating right? Marlo cooking for you?"

Bertha sneers. "Marlo doesn't cook."

"You could always go to Meals-On-Wheels. Victoria three doors down did. She says it's not too bad."

Bertha watches Stan, tells me later how graceful his long fingers are. Ed's were stubby, always rough.

"Says she's used to taking her hot meal at noon now," Betty continues. "Sandwich for supper."

Bertha leans forward.

"I said sand-*wich* for supper dear. Stan! Are you nearly done over there?"

"Oh, don't rush him Betty. Don't rush him at all. I'll have a bit more coffee—and a bagel if you have it. Cream cheese too."

"All right lovey then. Have you seen my dahlias this year? Double doubles. I can't understand it, dear. I mean look at this then."

Bertha stares at the bent-over Stan.

"Look, would you? It's a freak of nature it is. I mean the color is wonderful. All right lovey, I'll be right back with your coffee and bagel." Betty calls over to Stan, "I'll be right back Stanley—right back I will!"

Bertha stands and walks down the imaginary line between her place and theirs. A train trundles past on the far side of Bowness Road. Used to cross the Shouldice Bridge. The river is swollen at the bottom of the property. It swirls in a circle, forms a small vortex that makes a sucking noise as it flattens out and repeats itself. The willow bushes seem to reach out to the sound.

"Stan?" The sound of the shovel scraping is gone. "Stan!" Bertha calls. He walks away, metal pail half-full of cinders. "Let me," she says softly, hands on her chest just above her breasts as she jogs toward him.

"Don't worry at all ducks. I won't drop dead."

"Stan-ley, how could you say such a thing?" Betty sets the coffee and bagel on the table. "Here lovey. Don't pay him any mind."

Bertha seizes the opportunity, relieves Stan of the pail and walks away.

"Stan Smith. Well I never. That woman's husband died on the way to the bin."

Stan bites into the bagel and sips the fresh coffee; watches Bertha carry the cinders toward the front of her home.

47

≈≈≈

Inside Bertha's kitchen a fine mist dusts the air. The yellow ceramic counter top is covered with newspaper. Bertha sets the pail next to the urn containing Ed's remains. Pail and urn stand side by side like pre-measured ingredients. Bertha lines up her utensils: trowel, then ladle, then slotted spoon, then sieve.

She speaks to Ed as if he were sitting at the table by the window. "I'm taking the lid off and letting in a bit of air. It's been a while since you've had any fresh air."

She hesitates, but her hands are steady as she gently places the lid on the newspaper. "How does that feel? Feels okay to me," she says, peering inside.

She notices a few calcified lumps and pokes the surface of one with her forefinger. "I don't expect you've ever felt contained before. Of course you haven't. You were free to come and go as you pleased, really—able to concentrate on one thing at a time; able to focus your whole self. Well, now you're going to know how it is to divide yourself, how it is when your gut and your heart are separated, part required for mothering, part reserved for wife-ing, and the rest reserved for your lover."

Bertha eases the ladle into the urn, bends her wrist and fills the wide metal reservoir usually reserved for gravy. Her movements are slow and deliberate. "Easy now."

She opens a re-sealable plastic bag using her free hand and her teeth. The sandwich bag opens wider when she snaps it in the air. "There you are," she gently lets the dust line the bottom of the small sack.

She breathes loudly, palm in the middle of her chest. "The first attempt at something is always the toughest. That's what you always told me. The second attempt is easier, and so on. I think I understand what you meant now."

Bertha maneuvers the ladle in and out of the first bag six times, then quickly washes away the moisture that builds up on her palms. She fills three more bags. "I wonder what you'd think, if you could think."

She fills the fifth bag carefully, pouring the residue from the urn. "Not quite as much as in the other four—but looks okay—don't you think so? I mean it would be fabulous if you really could give yourself out evenly—but," she seals the bag between thumb and forefinger, "life doesn't always allow us that luxury—does it?"

She places each bag inside another so that the five individual pouches of ash are secured within a double wall of plastic. Then she lines the bags up in a sun-lit section of the counter. "No reason why you can't enjoy a bit of heat. I'll be right back. I need another pail."

Bertha retrieves an empty ice cream bucket from the garage and goes back to work, humming, dips the trowel in the bucket of fireplace ash and empties its contents into the sieve. She pats the side with her hand, encourages the finer bits to pass through the mesh like flour for her best piecrust. The lumps she reserves in a pile on the newspaper.

She fills the ice cream bucket in one hour and nineteen minutes, massages the back of her neck with both hands and decides on a glass of lemonade. After pouring, she sits at the table and thinks that the empty urn is truly hideous. Wide at the top, narrow at the bottom, the base color almost matches the fixtures in her lilac en-suite. The lid is edged in gold-colored paint and crowned by a gold knob. Yellow, pink and orange Gerber daisies blur the embossed surface, soften the finish. "What was I thinking," she says out loud. "I could have chosen a statue with a hollow base where I could keep part of you. The statue choices included two dolphins jumping glass waves, a ceramic angel holding a small steel ball, or a miniature of the CN Tower. I wish I'd chosen the memento chest, compressed sawdust finished to look like mahogany, the inside lined with simulated velvet. You, compressed and vacuum-sealed in a brick-sized temporary package, designed to fit inside. After sprinkling you in a meaningful place I could have used the box to organize your favorite fishing flies, or to hide the extra keys to the Rover, or to keep a small cutting from your best overalls, your favorite suit or pajamas. I should have chosen the memento box option. Marlo could've used the little chest for her wedding rings, better than the shoe box she uses now."

Bertha fills the urn with sifted fireplace ash and places it in the middle of her kitchen table. "Jesus Christ Almighty!" she exclaims. The five double-layered bags on the counter are swollen. Moisture beads the insides. Hands shaking, Bertha opens and deflates each bag. They sigh.

Chapter V

Bertha rarely drives, trundles her bike out of the garage when she comes to see me. She takes a look at the hard plastic helmet I insist she wears before yanking the wooden door shut. She hates electric garage door openers. Doesn't trust them. She straddles the frame, places a foot on the pedal and lifts her rear to the gel seat, one cycling innovation that she approves of.

"Comfy," she says out loud.

"Aye—comfy," Ed used to say in return.

She makes her way to the end of the cul-de-sac near the Shouldice Bridge. Forty years ago her block and the one next to it was open space. Now the same few acres house a collection of attractive semi-detached bungalow homes for mature adults. Well built. I chose the complex myself. The dividing and outer walls are brick, not wood.

"Old people," she says, pedaling along the pavement that runs parallel to the Bow River. While she rides she watches for the cracked molehills that disguise poplar roots, carefully avoiding bumps that threaten the contents of her pannier. There is a slight incline before the bend in the river where she likes to stop, where she and her Eddie liked to sit on the bench and stare across the water at the northwest wilderness. Her chest heaves when she reaches the top. She brakes. A young couple sits on the bench.

"Mor—ning," they singsong together.

She forces a smile, swallows a lump, and keeps going.

Bertha and Ed bought the big lot backing onto the Bow after they lived with Ed's mother for five years. Bowness was a new part of the city then. The path she rides on now was a hard-packed trail years ago; overgrown bushes and trees made the riverside a refuge. They spent a year clearing the lot before they built a small two-storey home with a veranda. The following year Ed added a shop to the property, a building big enough to hold four cars. Instead he filled it with tools and built cabinets. My parents didn't own a car then.

Later, I bought the property from them, kept the shop for Ed, parked my car where the Rover used to sit. That's about the time Ed retired and about the time I met Joel.

Bertha stops her bike and walks off the path to the low one-rung fence that edges the property now. She looks at the house I constructed around the original and sighs. "Nearly three thousand square feet of boxed air and not a grandchild in sight."

Ah, well, Ed would say, *never mind. You canny miss what you don't have.*

She grips the handlebars, breathes in, breathes out. "Here I am," she says, as she walks toward the gate. "My daughter thinks I need to let go, wants to take me traveling. I wonder if it's illegal to transport ashes across the International Date Line?"

She pats a double-layered zip-lock bag through the thickness of her fanny pack, rests her bike against the garage wall, and unlocks the door, welcomes the sight of Ed's toolbox. She walks toward the red metal container and gently rests the pannier bag on the workbench.

≈≈≈

I agonize for days over which tent to pack, the three-man or the two. The three-man is a domed affair with lots of headroom. Still holds that thick smell of the paraffin bug repellent that Thomas swore by. The two-man demands closeness: wide at the door, narrow toward the foot end. Joel had to cock his head sitting up in it. What bothers me most is the fact that they both have only one door.

"Coo-ee! I'm here," Bertha calls. The screen door in the kitchen slides back so hard that it jumps out of its track.

"Mother—"

"Sorry darling. I never do get that right."

I feel the muscle on the back of my arm jump as I watch her place the small plastic wheels back in the track and demonstrate just how slowly she can close the screen.

"Decided?" she asks.

"No."

"We are leaving in five days."

"I know."

"What's the problem?"

"No problem. I'm going to buy another one."

"Another tent?"

"Another tent."

"You have four."

"I'm wrestling with these two. The others are too heavy. I want something that's adaptable."

"I thought weight wasn't an issue in a canoe."

"I saw one yesterday with two doors." A tent that allows for escape.

"Two doors?"

"So that when you get up in the middle of the night you don't have to crawl over me."

"I'm your mother! But how heavy is this other tent?"

"It's very practical. It has two vestibules. Lots of gear space and I know I'll use it again."

"That's what you said about your last wedding dress."

"Help me stuff these back in the bags and we'll put them away."

We kneel together, rolling fabric homes into pack-away bundles. I feel the heat of the sun leave my back as I stand to take the tent bags upstairs, hear the

53

rush of the river across the hundred or so feet of lawn. The utility company claims it is not increasing the flow yet and the Lakes and Rivers engineer I spoke with yesterday, the one I'm getting to know on a first name basis, says that spring run-off hasn't yet reached its peak. But the river is bloated. Engorged.

Bertha stares around the room that was once Jack's study, a fly-tying room for Thomas, a shrine for Raj, and an ammunition store for Lynn, who insisted on keeping the double French door wide open to the elements. A tall wardrobe with three panels crosses the corner farthest from the door, map rack next to it. On the opposite wall five long shelves, about two and a half feet wide and six feet long, hold an assortment of outdoor shoes, ground sheets, fishing flies, containers and squeeze tubes, water bottles, a ceramic core filter with an extra carbon layer, a case of iodine drops, and a camouflage vest.

"Good God! I'll never get over the clutter in this room!"

"All useful," I reply, looking at the inventory. Climbing ropes, crampons, freeze-dried food, a set of twelve stainless steel forks, bottles of Aspirin, several courses of antibiotics in brown plastic containers, a case of jasmine-scented candles, three jumbo boxes of panty-liners, and a six month supply of birth control pills. Sleeping bags of varying loft are spread out on the bottom shelf. On the floor under them a series of Thermarests stack one on top of the other according to length.

"Are we using the bags that zip together?"

"I don't think so, Bertha."

In the other corner is an old coat stand that looks like a banana tree after a heavy rain, forty-three stuff sacks hang from its hooks.

"May I?" Bertha asks, slipping two fingers into the antique wardrobe handle.

My skin crawls.

Bertha turns the key in the old lock. "These dresses should be in bags, darling."

I rearrange the tents and an assortment of lifejackets in the middle of the floor. Hide behind my long hair. "Take off the fanny pack and try this one," I say.

I hold up a purple jacket with bright red cinch straps and a long belt that goes from the back to the front, through the legs.

"It would never fit me," Bertha says, gently hanging the fanny pack on the coat stand.

"Not the dress, the jacket."

"In a minute. Which is your favorite?"

"Don't have one. You know that."

"You spent—what—minutes deciding on these, remember?"

"No."

"You never took time to compare."

"Waste of time."

"*This* is my favorite." Bertha carefully pushes three dresses aside and reaches in to extract a full-skirted vapory version. Her arm circles the skirt, caresses it, and guides it toward the open door. She removes her arm and the skirt expands as if the fabric has a life of its own. "Pull that dress form over here," she says.

I adjust the shrunken shape until it matches Bertha's height. "Why not. I haven't looked at it for quite a while."

"It'll yellow if you don't wrap it up."

"It's not white anyway."

Bertha removes the long thin loops from the covered hanger. Instead of slipping the skirt over the form, she holds the strapless beaded bodice against herself. "Maybe I should get married again."

"Please."

"What? You think I'm too old? Unattractive? There's a young retiree in my Tai Chi class every Thursday who just might be suitable. I'm serious."

She zips the dress onto the form, expands the chest panels so that the dress doesn't fall to the floor and looks at me. "You must have felt like a princess in this."

"More like a fool."

Bertha tries on a tiara-style headpiece. She strikes a pose. I hold out the purple jacket. She turns and hooks her arms through. "Feels fine."

"Nope. Too short in the waist. It's not supposed to bind," I say, watching Bertha reach between her legs for the crotch strap.

"Is this a child's jacket? My God—are you trying to tell me something? I don't care if you're not married!"

I help her out of the jacket and turn to get another.

Bertha disappears into the wardrobe again. This time she retrieves a wispy pearl scarf and wraps it around her elegant neck—front to back to front, the ends grazing her shins. "Darling, is this how you wore this gorgeous stole?" The material underlines her face and softens the severity of her shorn white hair.

I hold up another PFD. "Put your arms in here."

"Perfect."

"Let me see," I say, cinching the three belts and checking the shoulders.

"Perfect."

"It fits, but I'm going to pick up an approved jacket."

Bertha looks puzzled.

"Turn."

Bertha turns her back to me, holds the long scarf in her hands slightly away from her sides. "Are you sure that's really required?"

I leave the room, and come back holding a roll of toilet paper. "No, but this is. I'm going to get an approved color, yellow or orange. That way if one of us falls in we'll be visible in the water. The one you're wearing is okay for water skiing."

"You know I hate one-ply."

"Walk around a bit. See how it feels. Make sure you'll have room to paddle."

Instead, Bertha squats and opens the drawer in the base of the wardrobe. "Oh, yes!" She balances and slips on a pair of beaded, square-toed, square-heeled, pearl-colored sling backs. "Why don't you at least wear the shoes? They are fantastic."

"Okay, I admit liking the shoes. It took me weeks to find them."

"Italian?"

"They're cloth. From that little village south of Stratford, remember? The costume shop next to the fishmonger?"

"No."

"You must. We went into the café next door on the other side and had peas and vinegar. That disgusting concoction you said you and Ed liked so much."

"I remember the peas and vinegar, but not the costume shop. A lot of details are missing in the month right after Ed's death. Unnatural isn't it?"

"Isn't what?"

"Not having someone to do for."

"Get rid of the scarf. It's cutting off the blood to your brain."

"I loved your father."

"I loved him too."

"I married him wearing a blue tweed suit and a pillbox hat."

"Blue tweed. I'll wear that next time. Remind me."

"Next time? Is there someone I don't know about?"

"Long red hair and a ponytail."

"What?"

"Look, she's right here," I say, holding the thickness of my hair away from my face.

"*What?*"

I turn Bertha to the mirror that lines the wardrobe door.

My mother scowls at my reflection. "Your trouble, my dear, is that no one is as perfect as you are."

I reach past Bertha and retrieve a shoebox from the shelf above the dresses. "Here," I say. "This will cheer you up. Your favorite part of the trousseau, milady."

She throws the lid on the floor. "Darling! The rings! So selfish to keep them locked up."

"I can't wear them."

"That doesn't make sense. Imagine the cost—they should be in a safety deposit box."

"No one will look in an old shoebox in a wardrobe in a house at the end of a street in Bowness."

"Marlo, let me put them somewhere for you. By the way, who gets these in the event that you—?"

"I'm giving them back."

"Giving them back?"

"Giving them back. Can't seem to get rid of them any other way."

"You could have done that right away instead of shutting them up in this rotting old closet."

Bertha kneels on the floor and opens a silver bell-shaped container that reveals a half-carat emerald-cut ruby. The stone is the color of old blood. She sets it reverently on the top shelf near the birth control pills. A square box ornately carved with elephants opens to reveal an unadorned wedding band and fifteen twenty-four carat gold bangles of varying widths. She places the box next to the silver bell, executes a reverse bowing motion.

She opens a small square of tissue paper, disclosing a wide ring made of white gold worked in a filigree pattern. As she places the ring next to the carved box she says, "White gold makes the twenty-four carat look dull. Where are the others?"

"I lost one—and the other—recently ruined my blender."

Bertha helps me return the contents to the wardrobe and we go outside.

"I just made another woman's day."

"How'd you do that?" Bertha asks.

"Sold her a house with a river view."

"Jesus, Mary, and Joseph. What'll you do with the cash this time?"

"I want to be sainted."

"Sainted?"

"Sainted. You know—"

"Like Mary or Veronica or Bernadette?"

"Somewhat like Bernadette—"

"You'll have visions? Your past and now martyred husbands will speak to you from the gazebo in the back yard? The spores on the lilies surrounding it will bleed and Bowness will be denoted on the tourist map of Calgary by an image of a flashing Sacred Heart?"

"You're getting carried away, Bertha."

"God love and preserve us, I wish I could be carried away."

I get up from the cedar chaise and go into the house. I watch Bertha as she looks towards the June rush of the Bow River, wonder if she notices how close the water line is to my garden.

She gets up, descends the four steps that run the width of the deck, and walks towards the garage. The closer she gets to the building, the quicker she moves. She walks through the side door and goes directly to the workbench under the window on the other side. The cement floor shoots cold into her sixty-three-year-old calves; she relishes the feeling. Reminds her of the chilblains she experienced as a child. She opens the lid of the small red toolbox, the one that contains the oldest and best used of Granda's bits and pieces. She lifts the tray-like portion to the side and draws comfort from the sight of the four small plastic sacks beneath.

I pad across the cement. "I'll have to put all that away sometime. I never have used the stuff Ed put in there."

Bertha slides the tray back into place and closes the lid.

"I love the way Ed was so neat," I continue. "Look at the spanners and the screwdrivers and the levels and the hammers and the saws and the planes. I love the way Dad planed, the rhythm of his movements—loved watching him."

"Bernadette of the visions is it then? Did my daughter actually make something to eat for her starving mother? Don't put it all away. That way it'll look as if there's a man about the place. What did you make me?"

"Fried bread."

"Tomatoes?"

"Tomatoes and eggs."

"Trying to bump me off? What did you make for yourself then?"

"A shake."

"A green barley shake? Marlo you've got to get over this thin stuff. Every time you meet a new man you adjust to fit his mould. I don't know how your body survives the piercing and the wrapping and the shaving and the hiking, the climbing, or the weeks in the wilderness. And what about the changes in religion?"

"Come on—let's eat. Religion is simply a way of life."

"Honest to God, when I think back, Raj was the best of the lot. He liked to see you with a bit of extra weight and you at least worshipped something spiritual with him. Jack—I don't know."

"He's an atheist—"

"And you know Ed hates him."

"Hated him."

"Every mention of the man's name makes your poor Dad turn over in his grave."

I hunch my shoulders and step in the middle of each carefully placed piece of flagstone between the garage and the house. "He's not in a grave."

"I mean mother of God, the man must weigh less than I do and he's at least a foot taller."

Bertha hurries her tiny frame, tries to walk next to me. She grazes her upper thigh on the arbour.

"Be careful. Jack knows how to keep everything in check."

"I don't remember how you met the idiot."

"Taking over for Ed, are you?" I wonder why she brings up Jack instead of Joel.

"I would have called him an ee-git then, now wouldn't I?"

"Let's talk about something else."

Our pace quickens as we reach the deck. Bertha places her hand on my arm and I turn on the first step and look down. "Mother of God, you're short."

"You never call me mother."

"Well, I'm going to start adding Theresa to that if you don't stop preaching to me."

"I thought saints liked that sort of thing—Veronica is it then? Get a towel and wipe the bloody sweat from my brow."

"Let's go in. It's cooler in the house."

"But the garden is green and lush and the tulips are full and the irises are ready to burst. Let's take lunch outside."

"Come and help me then. Your eggs are probably stone cold."

"No matter."

We go through the motions of setting the cedar table with cutlery, stoneware dishes, napkins, water goblets, a coloured glass pitcher of ice water, salt and pepper shakers and one of the smaller dried flower arrangements left over from Ed's memorial service. We trail back and forth like ants carrying crumbs. I place a tall blue glass full of green mixture in one place, add a plate full of fry-up to the other, and sit.

"You're actually going to drink that?" Bertha asks, adding a bowl of blueberries to the table.

"I am. Especially if you're going to eat that platter of grease-laden fatty matter."

"I grew up on fried bread. So did you."

I choke. Green liquid spurts from my nostrils.

"Fried bread and butter balls."

61

"I don't remember any of that," I say, smearing the napkin in my hand. "I think you're making it up."

"Ed loved to make you butter balls—a knob of butter rolled in sugar. You ate them after school." Bertha's fingertips shine as she pulls her bread apart. "You and your friend Josephine."

My throat constricts at the thought. This time I take a smaller sip.

"Isn't she dead now as well?" Bertha asks.

"Yes."

"Single car wreck—right?"

I watch Bertha dunk her bread in the runny yolks. "Too many butterballs," I say.

"Don't speak ill of the dead!"

The egg whites stare up at me like a face without eyes. "They might hear me?"

"Might visit just to set the record straight."

"Of course! If I bump into someone on my way to the bathroom in the dead of night, I'll know *she's* come." A few more swallows and I'll be done.

"She had a lovely funeral."

"Lovely?" The drink is vile. I ogle the blueberries.

"Lovely," Bertha says. "Remember the dress her mother bought for her? Must have cost a few hundred dollars. And that was a lot of money in nineteen-eighty. All that lace and those frills. Italians are mad about it."

"Something Josephine wouldn't have been caught dead in."

"There she was. Laid out like an ugly bride. Head covered by a chest-length veil you couldn't see through. I never did figure out the neckline, bouquet of orchids. What was her mother thinking?" The last of the crust disappears between Bertha's lips.

"I can't believe you looked, Bertha."

"It's disrespectful not to."

"I wanted to remember her with her head on."

"Jesus Christ!"

I reach for the remaining tomato half and sink my teeth into it. "That's why it was covered up. That's why the coffin was only open for the prayers—closed for the funeral."

"I knew you couldn't stomach that green stuff!" Bertha says. "Here, have the egg whites as well!"

I stare at my mother and swallow the last of the shake. We take turns plucking the blueberries from the bowl, popping them into our mouths. Move back and forth like kids on a seesaw.

"Have you decided about Ed?" I ask.

"You don't have to push me."

"Sorry."

"No you're not."

"He can't live in the bathroom forever."

"Why not? The urn looks great on the edge of the Jacuzzi."

"It's strange—you told me you hate that thing."

"The bathroom was Ed's favourite room. Spent hours in it."

I begin piling the dishes. "Put the woodworking magazines away yet?"

"No—but I cleaned up the *Car and Driver* issues. Must have been three years worth stacked on either side of the pedestal sink."

"You humoured him far too much."

"You can never humour a husband too much! Where's your head? I let him pile magazines in the loo—"

"And in the kitchen, the living room, the laundry room, and the entrance."

"So what—at least I ate what I wanted."

"Touché. Help me carry this stuff in, would you?"

"I'm the guest, am I not?"

I sit down again. "You're right, Bertha. It's beautiful right here. Everything in the garden is fantastic." We take in the steep brown banks on the other side of the Bow. "I haven't even fertilized yet and I have the greenest lawn on the block."

"So how did you—bump into Jack again? Last I heard he moved to Montreal."

"I was just starting to enjoy your company."

"Okay, I've decided that Ed should be interred," she says.

"I met him when Nemit had nude photos taken for her partner."

"The lesbian woman? I'm not going with Queen's Park. It's too expensive. Nude?" she asks.

"Completely."

"Well—I think Edenbrook is better. Scenic. Mountain views."

"Not as if he'll see anything, Mum. Cheaper?"

"Yes. But we will when we visit. Doesn't it bother you that a man you are now dating—if that's what you call seeing an ex-husband—was taking photos of a nude woman?"

"We're not dating. I had some unfinished business with him—and he's a photographer. You know how I feel about monuments to the dead. I don't think there's any point."

"So you'll come to the interment?"

"Why aren't we sprinkling him?"

"Where would we do that?"

"Over the mountains. I thought he loved that helicopter trip into Assiniboine."

"Are you kidding? He threw up. Besides, he'd end up in our faces if we tried to empty him over a ledge. Even I know something about updrafts, Marlo."

"What about the river?"

"The river?"

"The Bow."

"No."

"Why not?"

"So were you turned on or something?"

"What?"

"Watching Jack take pictures of the naked lesbian."

"Why can't we sprinkle Ed in the Bow?"

"He'd be washed away. Were you?"

"What do you think?"

64

"I don't want to think about it. I just wish you could understand my need to—keep him."

"Keep him?"

"You know how men are about things that last."

"Blowhard?"

"I knew you'd get tired of men sooner or later and go through a transformation. That would explain Jack! He's just a front, isn't he?"

"Okay, I'll come to the interment! But don't expect me to visit a buried urn."

"I'm planning for the fifteenth of July."

"Why?"

"I want a procession."

"I was turned on, okay?"

"I don't care. You're going to be in it, headlights on, and hazards flashing. Were you really?"

≈≈≈

I struggle to have whole conversations with Bertha but we always get off track. I try to tell her about Jack that day, tell her that he wants to sue me, planning to take half my holdings, but we don't get that far.

"Have you ever met a man who is completely in love with himself?" I ask Bertha.

"Jesus Christ—in love with himself? You mean as in adoring himself frequently?" Bertha gestures as if she's rolling something back and forth between her open palms.

"Self-love, as in taking absolute care of the body—"

"All men are like that Marlo. Five husbands and you still don't know that the peni—"

"I'm talking about physicality."

"So am I!"

"I'm trying to tell you about Jack." We stand in front of the deep kitchen sink, arms three-quarters submerged in soapy water.

"Look Marlo," Bertha continues. "All those times that you thought those men were turned on by your natural beauty, they were just turned on."

"Have I ever told you how many times you twist—?"

"The story before you even get the chance to—"

"Let me tell it, then! Don't wring the sleeping bag like that! You'll ruin the loft."

Water spills over the edge of the marble counter, runs down the white lacquered cabinet and drenches the front of our pants. I use a mop to soak up the puddles on the hardwood floor, stand on a towel, take off my jeans, and pad across the floor to the patio door. Bertha watches me throw the jeans over the clothes dryer. When I come back, she hands over her light blue cotton pants.

"So you said you were turned on when you met Jack." She stares at my bare buttocks as I stride across the lawn.

"Are you finished squeezing the water out?" I ask, over my shoulder.

"No. Sorry." Bertha snaps the elastic on the leg of her Lycra underwear. "I'll go back in. Squeeze softly."

I'm ankle deep in the water-saturated lawn when Earl coughs to announce his arrival.

"Looks like the seepage is up another foot or so since yesterday," he says.

I turn slowly to face him, cross my arms.

"What is the Department of Lakes and Rivers going to do about this, Earl? It is Earl isn't it?" I move toward him, wiping my feet on a dry section of grass. He backs up, eyes fixed on something about six inches to the left of my hips.

"I came to drop this off."

I take a thick, perfect-bound government booklet. "*Erosion Control Programs*," I read.

"Kind of dry," he says. "Lots about compensation if it comes to that." He turns around completely as I head towards the house. "Read the 'Policies' section!" he yells, shoulders shaking, unable to contain his laughter.

"Who was that?"

"Earl," I say when I go back inside.

"Earl?"

"Have you noticed how high the water is? The department of Lakes and Rivers have been around almost daily. Jesus Bertha, you've already soaked everything within a ten-foot radius." The counter surrounding the sink, the ledge in the bow window and the floor are drenched.

"I'll clean it up this time. What about out there?" she asks, pointing the dripping mop. "Have they talked about sandbagging?"

"All Earl talks about is how lush my garden is." I empty the sink and scoop the dripping bags into a plastic tub, soaking the front of my legs.

"I don't know why you don't just send the sleeping bags to the dry cleaner," Bertha says.

"Come on."

"But my pants."

"Don't worry, he's gone!"

Water dribbles up my arms as we hoist the bags and stretch them across the clothes dryer.

"Thought you were going to take my whirligig out when you moved in here. Not very sophisticated, you said."

"I'm sentimental."

"Sentimental?"

"I used to peg the clean sheets together, stake them out like a tent."

"How could I forget?"

We walk the hundred and thirty feet to the bottom of the garden. The last twelve and a half are underwater. "What I don't understand about this is that my neighbour's lawns aren't showing any signs of seepage."

"This water is warm," Bertha says, swishing her toes from side to side as if she's on a beach.

"Look at the ground a little way along the bike path." Grass sticks out of large patches of dry ground here and there. "The city is going to close this section of the path if the water gets any higher."

Three houses downstream the river no longer laps over the bank.

67

~~~

We talk about Jack again during mass, three days later. "Jactitation."

"You can't say ejaculation in Church!" Bertha hisses.

"Jactitation," I repeat.

"Jack-tit-ation? He's in love with your non-existent breasts?"

We kneel, elbows on the pew in front. Communion is still being served and the St Bernard choir is belting out a guitar-laden version of *Nearer to My God Am I*.

"It's a sort of restlessness," I say. We are having our weekly, behind-the-missal conversation.

"And this connects to?"

"The day I met Jack again."

"Hmm. Not another adjectified man."

"I don't objectify anyone." I smile at the communicants returning from the altar with chalices of unredeemed host.

"Adjective, adject-fied—Domenic?"

"Domenic?"

"The Domenizer—"

"Will you get over that? I was nineteen."

"Over and done."

The priest sits when he returns the chalice to the tabernacle and the congregation moves as one from the kneelers to their seats. We are still kneeling.

"Then don't bring him up!" I hiss.

A young child in the row in front turns and laughs out loud. His mother grabs his arm, glares at me, and turns him back.

"So the day you met Jack," Bertha whispers. We sit back.

I lower my voice. "I was experimenting—with the blender."

"Another color shake?"

"Not exactly. How the hell did you pick up on Dom having anything to do with this? I was trying to get rid of something—"

The priest rises and moves to the pulpit. "Let us give thanks to the Lord our God for the gift of his sacrament." The congregation stands.

"You've never been able to make a straight point with me," Bertha whispers.

"It's no wonder," I say. "I'm liquidating."

"But you've already sold the property you had with Jack, right?"

"Right. Doubled down and used the money to assume the mortgages on the two Montgomery places I told you about. I wanted to get rid of the ring. I'll never wear another one as long as I live."

"This week's announcements begin with prayers for the sick of our parish—"

"Please," Bertha says.

"I tried leaving it in a coffee shop when I met Nemit before the photo session. I left it in the space between two spindles in the back of a wooden chair."

"So you *lost* it?"

"We left the shop and I was getting into my car when the bus boy ran up and gave it back."

"Blessed be God," Bertha says.

"Please stand for the final blessing."

"I've never seen you like this," she goes on.

"Mass is ended. Go forth to love and serve the Lord!"

"So then you went home and put the ring in the blender?" she asks. "Let's go before the final hymn."

"Too late. No—before I met Nemit for coffee, I listened to the thing jump around while I crushed ice for a drink. Very satisfying."

"Please turn to hymn number 433, *How Great Thou Art*."

"Christ, Marlo! Where is it now?"

"Embedded in my car tire."

"Let me guess."

"I don't think you could."

"You've intentionally driven over a one-and-a-half carat diamond and embedded it in the tire of your sport utility vehicle?"

"I sold that two days ago."

"So the ring is a bonus gift for the person who bought the vehicle you owned with Raj?"

"Raj bought the vehicle."

"I thought he left the country?"

"He did. I sold the truck through a consignment dealer. The one that turns over all the vendor vehicles for Symmetry Real Estate Brokers. His name is on the paperwork they returned to me. I think he bought the truck for a family member."

"*They'll* never find it. Some unsuspecting tire changer is going to strike it rich."

"No. It's embedded in the tire of my new car."

The woman in the pew in front glares, grabs her son by the hand, pushes past her neighbors, and marches up the aisle followed by two other children.

"Car?"

"A nineteen sixty-eight MG Midget."

"Christ in heaven," she says.

The congregation's voice tapers off at the end of the second verse and the choir sings the chorus again by itself. The priest, celebrants, and altar boys begin their procession out.

"Is this the first time you tried to wreck a ring?" she continues.

"A month ago I walked to the high school grounds to see Nemit's son play baseball."

"Ah, yes. The lesbian son. What's his name again?"

A man in the pew behind us coughs.

"Adam. You know that. I was just sitting there, cooling off after the long walk, fingering the platinum setting when Adam asked me to help him warm up." We move to the end of the pew and genuflect before turning to leave.

"What position does he play?"

"Pitcher."

"Adam, pitcher on the Bowness junior baseball team. Son of Nemit, the lesbian in the nude Jack photographs." The crowd around us dissipates.

"So I catch for him," I continue. "When the coach yells, *Balls in!* I let the ring fly."

"To the pitching mound?"

"No. I wanted to show off so I tossed the ball out to the kid in right field. I felt—" We skirt the outer edge of the crowd, avoiding Father Joe's sweaty Sunday palm.

"Relieved?"

"Satisfied." Outside the damp air engulfs us.

"Your hair is a frizzy mess," Bertha says.

"The kid was busy digging the toes of his brand new cleats into the dirt. I thought he wasn't paying attention. He let the ball go by, looked as if he completely misjudged the direction. The coach yelled at him to get the ball and come in. He left the ball where it landed and ran in, wind-milling his arms. Three days later Nemit called and said the coach asked all the parents if someone lost a ring. Nemit recognized the ring and called me. What can I say? I phoned the coach, gave a description. Nemit picked it up for me."

"That's unbelievable."

"Some kid speared the ring with a cleat."

"I think you should pray."

"We were just in church."

"To Saint Jude."

"Saint Jude?"

"The prayer to St Jude. Say it faithfully for seven days. Favors are given if public recognition is promised."

"As in the *Thank you St. Jude for prayers answered* lines in the paper? Next to the legal and judicial notices?"

"As in *Prayer Corner.*"

"I don't believe it. What do these people pray for? Miracles? Money? Love?"

"Death," she says. "I mean, I suppose you could pray for death. Probably peace of mind, the safety of a loved one, the return of a lost item."

"Rain."

"You would do that."

In the parking lot we stand on opposite sides of the Rover. The woman upset by our conversation during mass spins gravel and almost crashes into a passing car. Bertha fiddles with the keys.

"What do you think upset her most, us talking, or us discussing the destruction of a perfectly good wedding ring?" she asks.

"Ring."

"Why?" Bertha mouths from inside the gray car as she reaches for my door handle.

"She was at mass without a husband," I say.

Bertha turns the key in the ignition and backs out of the stall. She steers the car away from the church and turns toward the Trans Canada.

"Where are we going? I thought we were going to visit auntie."

"I want to show you the procession route," she says.

"Ed's been gone for six months. Don't people only do that kind of thing the day of the funeral?"

"It's important to me."

"He would be mortified."

"He's upset that I never did that after his funeral."

"I don't believe that, Bertha. I think it's just your imagination. I think what you are feeling is just good old Catholic guilt."

"There's a difference between regular guilt and Catholic guilt?"

"Of course! Catholicism depends on guilt. Priests are conditioned to make people feel bad about deviating even slightly from established rituals. Reason I never married in a church."

"This is a conversation you should be having with Ed."

I put my hand on her arm. "He's dead, Mum," I say in a gentle voice.

"Not to me. Not to me," Bertha gulps.

The silent car glides up Sarcee Trail hill. I open and close the zipper on my purse; the noise seems to echo off the teak dashboard.

"Pay attention," is the first thing Bertha manages to say. "You always get lost and refuse to look at a map. You're just like your Dad."

"He asked for directions. I know where Edenbrook is."

"*You* don't seem to know how to follow them."

"I'm like you then."

The car curves west onto Seventeenth Avenue and regains speed without the lurch that accompanies gear changes in domestic models.

"How much did Ed pay to bring this car from Glasgow?"

"About as much as I paid for his funeral."

"That's all?"

Bertha brakes at the last set of lights before we leave the city. "I knew you thought I didn't spend enough!"

"That's not what I mean and you know it." I look ahead at the narrow up and down tarmac. "I don't know why you're upset."

"Upset?" Bertha stomps her foot on the accelerator.

"Every time we discuss Ed—the closer we get to the cemetery, the grumpier you are."

"You are being completely disrespectful now," she says, voice quivering.

"Of you?" I ask.

"Of the whole process," she says.

"Well it makes you strange." My stomach lurches as the Rover crests the first hill. "You're driving too fast!"

"Jesus." She eases her foot off the pedal.

"What are you thinking? What makes you like this?"

"I haven't had an orgasm in nine months, three weeks, two days and eleven hours," she says. "What do you expect?"

"Bertha, that's not it."

"How do you know? You just go from man to man to man!"

"I think we should leave this for another time."

"We can't. You are probably already *with* that Jack again. I've sent out invitations for a lunch."

74

"You want me to help you?"

"I don't *need* your help Marlo." We approach the intersection that leads into the cemetery. Bertha brings the car to an easy stop. "I suppose you'll be bringing him?" she asks.

"You're getting carried away. I'm not seeing him."

"Oh, so he's not the kind who is respectful of family rites?"

"Family rites?"

"Of passage. Look, there's the Catholic area."

"Segregated dead people?"

"Let's get out and look," she says. "The Garden of Remembrance. I want to show you the plot."

How quaint, I think. I open the door and swing my legs to the ground. "It's not exactly a plot is it? I mean it's only a foot square."

"Close the door, would you?"

I walk across the grass, trying not to let the cube heels of my new Italian shoes sink in the softness. In front of me is a large white rectangular marble monument; it's twelve feet wide and five feet high. I rarely need to measure a room in the homes I buy and sell. In an alcove at its center, a bronze statue of the Virgin Mary spreads her arms, palms open, head slightly bowed. I bend to read the commemorative message. When I realize it's in Latin I lift my head. The roof of the Rover enters my line of forward vision. I straighten up and watch Bertha circle to the gate and drive off.

I walk to the ornate bench that lets visitors preside over the small field of ground level plaques. I stand on it. No sign of the car on any of the three roads leading away from the gate, just a huddle of people a couple of gardens over. I decide that the novena to Saint Jude may not be such a bad idea. I wonder if I can remember all the words to the *Hail Mary* and the *Our Father*, which are supposed to precede it. I realize I should have prayed the day I met Jack again.

Chapter VI

The unmistakable reverberation of the automatic shutter is the only sound Jack hears. He ignores the bass drawl of the stereo and the prattle from the manager. His lens seeks intimacy with the woman waving in the simulated wind; the aperture is set to capture the hair on her forearms. She is a bag of translucent bones straining against a thin cover. He is disappointed she didn't come alone. The music stops and he kills the lights. *Thanks Jack*, she mouths before standing and allowing her manager to steady her, move her to the dressing room.

Jack has half an hour. He shuts off the oscillating blades and changes the backdrop to black. He drags a patterned green chaise across the room and sets it about two feet in front of the backdrop. Rosewood. Queen Anne legs bowed to the floor. In the kitchen he watches from the large window as the model slides onto the front seat of the manager's car and says, "Great idea." He recently turned the yard behind his Fifteenth Avenue home into paid parking space.

When he comes back from Montreal he calls to ask if I'll help him find a place. I decline. "Outside my territory," I say.

Most of the main floor of the house is studio. The second floor houses his bedroom, bathroom, and living room. The basement contains his office, darkroom and photo stock. Every room parallels his Spartan look, gaunt and austere.

He examines his hollowed cheeks in the distortion of the stainless eye-level wall oven, moves his head to admire his own symmetry. He sniffs twice before snipping the top off a pink pack of aspartame sweetener, empties its contents under his tongue. He ingests solids Friday, Saturday, and Sunday, purges Monday, Tuesday, and Wednesday. Thursday he rests.

When Nemit arrives, swinging a paper bag oozing a burger and plastic cheese aroma, he says, "No food."

I retreat to the hood of my small British convertible and let Jack stare as I mulch and swallow. I imagine the smell on his upper lip and picture him holding back the urge to scream. He moves away from the kitchen window and into the studio.

"I'm doing this as a gift," Nemit says.

"You explained when you called."

"For my partner," she goes on.

"That her?" he sneers.

"Not funny, Jack. I want something artistic. Something tasteful."

"Put your elbow there. Arm. Hand on your head. Look past the camera."

I watch Jack back away while Nemit stands up.

"This isn't it. Not what I want. Shoot my back."

"Your back?"

"My back."

Jack drags the chaise away and replaces it with a square table. Drapes it with black cloth. "Sit." Nemit sits. "Turn." She turns. "Hands there and there," he says. She grips the edge of the table on either side of her knees. "Elbows straight." She pushes up through her palms. "Look to the left." She looks left. "Gaze at the ceiling." She lifts her chin. Bluish shades strain over the shape of her spine, her square chin and the wings forming her shoulder blades. I've always admired her strength and accepted her weaknesses, watched her crumble when Joy cheats.

"Look right," Jack says. She looks right. "Stare at your *friend*." She stares hard.

The shutter ricochets until she laughs herself bent. The loose skin that covers her stomach folds like a Roman shade.

Jack changes the light. "Blue on black," he says.

"Why not white on black?" I suggest. My voice surprises him. "White on black," I repeat.

He drags the covered table away and replaces it with the chaise. "Lie on your side this time," he says. "Other hand toward your thigh. Knees slightly bent. Good."

"Good?" She says, straining to look over her shoulder.

"Look up," he says.

"Looking up."

The shutter speaks. I watch, comb my hand through my long hair, rake loose strands to the floor. The camera spins towards me.

"Sit for the last few shots," Jack says.

Nemit moves to the open end of the chaise. I can feel Jack's mood lifting.

"Right hand at the nape of your neck. Left stretched out to the side. Reach! Look at your thumb. Good!"

"Great," I say.

"That's it," Jack says as the shutter grinds to a full stop.

I wrap Nemit in a robe. The shutter makes one last leap. I purse my lips at his thin frame.

While I wait for her to dress, Jack moves back and forth between camera and kitchen. Retrieves a canister. Unloads a film. Finds a pen. Applies a label. Writes a name. Marches to the fridge. Opens the stainless door.

"No food?" I say.

"No."

"Don't eat?"

"You know my routine," he says, as if he enjoys the sealing sound of the door.

79

I cross my arms and lean against the end of the kitchen counter. "Roommates?" I ask. I see cheese and bread and wine before the door closes completely.

"You're kidding."

"Just making conversation. A friend? A woman?"

"A man," he says, evaluating my build.

Nemit emerges from the bathroom where she dressed. She trails her coat.

"You're worse than your kid!" I say.

"I'm high, my arms feel light," she replies.

"Probably from holding them up," Jack says.

"Let's go," Nemit says to me. "Thank you *Mr.* Bennet."

"Ten days," he says, before she asks.

He watches us, arms joined, heads touching, talk our way back to the car. We separate to open the doors and disguise our bodies behind its mustard frame.

≋

I'm in the garage, screwdriver in hand, when Bertha opens the side door and barges in.

"Hi!"

"Hello."

"Fixing something?" Bertha asks loudly, eyeing Ed's toolbox.

"Just tightening the mirror."

"This thing is pretty small, Marlo."

"Pretty small."

"Really small. Probably fit under an SUV."

"Probably."

"Did you get the ring out of your tire?" Bertha asks.

I concentrate on the screw head. Don't want to scratch the paint. "Damaged?" she goes on.

"Completely flat by the next day."

"I thought you could only do that to diamonds in cartoons!"

"The tire."

"You told me I'd never guess. So. How?"

"How what?" Do you ever catch yourself being nasty with your mother? I want to scream, but I know I'll only hurt myself.

"How did it—the ring—how did the ring become attached to the tire?"

"God damn it, Bertha!" I scream anyway.

"I don't think he did."

"Embedded!" I yell. "It was embedded in the tread! Nemit dropped it and I backed over it!"

"When?" she says calmly.

"When she came over to give it back! She walked up the driveway as I opened the garage door. She dropped it. I backed up. I stopped on top of it. She had an incredibly frightened look on her face. Then she started laughing. I asked, *what's wrong?* She just pointed. I got out. She said, *The ring.* I jumped in the car and spun the tires driving forward. That did it. Embedded the ring in the tire."

"Still there?" she asks.

"*Just* the setting," I say.

"The diamond?"

I expect her to ask about the diamond. "It fell out. Look at this." I point to the right rear tire with the screwdriver. The misshapen platinum can be mistaken for a squashed soft drink tab.

"But why is it still in there?"

81

"The flat tire was because of a leaky valve. I'm leaving it there. Feels—"

"Good?"

"Satisfying!"

"It's a feeling I know well," Bertha says, with a half-grin.

I throw the screwdriver. It lands noisily on the tray in the red toolbox.

"I'm sure you do."

"Careful with that."

"It's not going to break, Bertha—coming in?"

"Think I better ride home before it rains," she says.

"Suit yourself."

"The water's still high."

I move toward the side door and Bertha circles toward the workbench. "Still high. You don't need to fuss with that," I say as she stands in front of the toolbox.

"I'll just close the lid."

"Alberta Environment was out again today."

"On a Saturday?"

"Look, I have to go in because I'm expecting a call about the Inglewood house at two."

"What did they say about the water level?" she asks, still facing the wall behind the workbench.

"The purchaser isn't worried."

"Not the water level in Inglewood—the water level here."

"He got into explaining about water tables and aquifers."

"But they must be releasing more west of us in anticipation of the June run-off."

"There's surprisingly little headwater in the Spray lakes. It's not the utility company."

"Then what?"

"There's the phone." I run toward the house, leaving my mother where she is.

When Bertha hears the patio door slide to a close she opens the toolbox. The plastic sacks that she hid inside a few weeks before are intact. She decides they need to be moved and climbs up on the workbench, opens the cupboard above it. Thinks I don't go in there.

She transfers the small sacks. The last one is still in her hand when she hears me slide the screen door open. She lifts the last sack, rests it beside the others on the shelf above her head, and grabs a few paintbrushes as I come through the door. "Thought I'd paint the bathroom this coming week," she says, holding up an assortment.

"Aren't you having company on Thursday?"

"Saturday. A wheeler-dealer like you ought to know the date, dear."

"Don't get distracted or you'll fall and break something."

"My bones are better than yours."

"You know why I can't eat dairy."

"Yep. That man. Saturday is the fifteenth. You know that, right?"

I'm quiet. "Let me give you a hand down."

"You are coming, right? I'm not afraid of heights."

"You know how I feel about this ridiculous procession idea. Besides, I don't want to be left out there again."

"Afraid of ghosts, Marlo?"

"Get down yourself."

Bertha turns and thrusts the brushes back in the cupboard, slams the door.

"I mean, why can't we just drive out and do it? Why must we invite all those people? Ed wouldn't care," I say, surprised by the slight rise in my own voice.

Bertha squats and then awkwardly sits on the workbench. Her legs dangle about a foot off the floor.

"You are going to be filthy," I continue.

"Ed always cleaned up the workbench. I'm fine. So what if my cycling shorts are dirty."

I watch my mother jump down and smile.

"Are you coming on Saturday or not? I need to know," she says, adjusting her padded seat and pulling the spandex legs closer to her bony knees. The back of her dark green riding shorts is dusty and her hands look as if she's been reading the paper for a couple of hours.

"I'd rather you spend the rest of the week fuming."

"I guess that answers it."

"Where did you get those shorts?"

"At the cycling shop where you got me that ridiculous helmet." Bertha marches past me to her bike, which rests on the grass. "Shit. I left it standing."

"Don't worry; the grass couldn't have hurt it."

Bertha yanks the small frame upright. "The ground is soggy—I don't think it was quite like that when I got here. You better get the City to do something."

"Alberta Environment."

"The whole place is going to be submerged soon." We walk the length of the yard, both looking around at the burgeoning bushes. "That willow is taking over," she says. She's right. The hanging branches have tendrils that sweep the lawn. "You might have a root problem this year."

"I'll come for the lunch," I say, opening the gate and stepping through into the puddle on the other side. "Don't worry. I still have the Roto-Rooter number."

"Good thing you're wearing old sandals," she says, looking at my feet, which seem distorted under the water. "They went out of business years ago. I swear that tree is bigger every time I come here."

"What do you want me to bring?"

"Don't knock yourself out, Marlo."

Then she launches herself into the seat and pushes down hard on the pedals, sprays her own back with water.

"You're going to look like a skunk by the time you get home!" I call. I don't know why I always give in to that woman. *Becuz she's yer muther*, echoes in my head. "And where's your damn helmet?"

I plod back up the yard and close the garage door. Inside the house I sit on the floor rubbing my feet and eyeing the cover of the water management document. I check off the sections that pertain to my situation: "Grant Assistance," which I already know is up to sixty-five percent of the eligible costs to a maximum of two hundred and seventy five thousand, the "Special Policies" section, and the "Process" section. Just one tiny problem: the regulations are intended to compensate rural property owners.

I arrange a meeting with a prospective purchaser at the house in Inglewood. A graphic designer thinking of moving her business away from the old Dominion Steel warehouses on Twenty-fifth Avenue near Barlow Trail.

"Can't face another summer downwind of the stockyards," she says on the phone. The City zoning policies will allow for a business on New Street. That's not a problem. *Closer to downtown, easier access and better air*, were other reasons that the woman gave. *Don't want to rent any more*, was another. She couldn't know, but that was the only reason she had to give.

Two forty-five. I arranged to meet the woman at four-thirty. I run the water for a shower then stand in front of the full-length mirror in my bedroom. The scale's electronic voice says, "You lost 9.63 pounds." I look at what Jack would criticize. My abdomen is distended. I've definitely lost that soft outer coating that I've been nursing for the past few years. Nine pounds is significant tonnage when you are five feet two inches tall. Bertha thinks I'm too thin. Auntie Jane will say the same thing next Saturday. Reed will scoff like he always does. I look at my back. Not as good as Nemit's. Can't quite see the vertebrae yet but I see shadows under my skin. Only a slight hint of a single cellulite dimple on my left cheek. I cross the room, enter the steam and close the shower door.

≈≈≈

The woman is late. The door of her seven-seater vehicle opens over top of the MG.

"You'll have to get used to parking your vehicle on the street," I say.

"I thought I could maybe take the property next door as well, put a driveway on the side of the house and put up a garage in the back yard," she replies.

The automobile is a cross between a truck and a sport utility vehicle. Its wheel wells are level with my underarm. I stand next to it waiting impatiently for the woman to wrestle a briefcase from behind the driver's seat.

"Marlo Gilman," I say.

"Nice to meet you, Murlo."

"Marlo."

"I'm excited to go through the place and I have to tell you that I'm ready to write the cheque today. So let's talk numbers."

The woman follows me to the rear of the house. The grass is overgrown at the side, thigh-high clumps interspersed with dry patches of gray dirt.

"The yard will have to be dredged up. I can see it leveled out and divided by more planters, built in varying levels using treated posts. The ground will be covered with red shale."

"That's a possibility," I say.

The woman follows me to the edge of the property, which borders the river for about twenty yards. She looks at the top of my head and stares curiously at the collar of my Mandarin style dress.

"You are not at all what I expected. I'm Pauline Kaiser. I got your name from a friend who has some property near Point Mackay. Facing out to the water and the bike paths. There isn't one here, is there?"

"No. It switches to the north side at the old Zoo Bridge."

"He said you never advertise. He said you don't even carry a cell phone. How can you do business like that? Not many successful people who don't take up the technological advantages of the new millennium. Do you have a PC?"

I laugh. "Yes, Pauline, I have a PC. Use it to track property and prospective clients."

"You shop for clients?"

"I match people and properties."

"Most matchmakers are only interested in marrying their friends off."

"The contracts I'm involved in *are* a bit like marriage agreements," I say, looking up at the woman from below my lashes. "Let's go inside." My voice drops an octave. "I'm dying to know what you think of the interior."

"Does no one water right now? This yard feels like cement. I'll definitely have to do something with the building." The back profile of the house is aged wood siding. "Now why is it that the previous owner just upgraded the front of the house? Ran out of dough before he got done?"

"Moved to a drier climate. I can recommend an individual who specializes in restorations—"

"For the right price I might just raze the thing and start over."

"—or contemporary exteriors."

I open the door and we step into a three by three area. Stairs lead up to the kitchen.

"Where's the basement?"

"There isn't one. Just a root cellar outside."

"I thought that wood contraption was covering an electrical box."

"No."

"Now the only reason I'd be interested in keeping it original is if it's a miniature of the Deane house. That is an interesting place."

"The kitchen contains cupboards with a flat profile," I say. "Light colored wood, steel handles."

"Well I certainly wouldn't expect this from the outside. Oh, I love *that!*" she says, looking at the huge door hanging from a track on the ceiling.

"It's a coat closet."

"Very eclectic."

"If you'll move into the kitchen I'll close the outside door and you can see it properly," I say.

The woman moves her bulk up three stairs.

"Slide it back for me—exquisite," she says, about the shelves and coat rack that are revealed. "Although you'd need a stepladder to get up there." The bottom of the closet is about three feet above the floor.

I reach in and pull out a four-tier ladder, which folds out in an A-frame.

"Who'd want to climb that all the time? What did the last owner do?" she asks.

"He's an architect."

"He must have run out of money for sure," Pauline says, looking at the uncovered cement under my feet.

"The front entrance is the same," I say.

"Christ." Pauline opens a few of the tall kitchen cupboards. The doors extend to the ceiling. "What are these made of?" She asks, admiring a second sliding track door over the pantry.

"Plywood."

"No way! This has to be maple."

"Stained plywood," I say.

She runs her hand across the stainless counter top and admires the separate sinks which angle out from the corner to the left of the kitchen window.

"It's very cold, isn't it?"

"Depends what you like, I suppose," I reply, thinking of how much time Joel and I spent finishing the house.

"The floor is all right," Pauline arcs a foot over the dark square panels. "I don't think I've seen wood panels before. Are they a pre-finished product?"

"It's a cork floor. Easy on the cook," I say.

"Isn't that a fire hazard?"

"It has a retardant coating."

"I see."

"Let's move into the living room."

"Oh, I love that curved wall," Pauline exclaims. "Now that's architecture."

"The last owner didn't do that," I say. "The owner before did."

"Go figure. Don't like the cement surround on the fireplace either. You're right; it's at the front as well. What kind of furniture did he have in here?"

"Black leather."

"Jesus, I shiver just standing here. This is not at all like the Deane House. What the fuck was Andrew thinking about?"

"Perhaps he wanted to play a joke."

"On me? I don't think so. Christ. What's the upstairs like?"

"Actually there are two more rooms on this floor."

Pauline follows me across gleaming hardwood, past the curved wall. Its inside encloses a tiny room.

"What'd he use this for?"

"Drawings. He stored them in here in racks."

"And this one?"

"His office." There is a smaller version of the suspended track door between the two rooms.

"Christ, couldn't swing a cat in here! I hope the upstairs is better."

I lead her up a metal spiral staircase. Pauline moves carefully so that her expansive jeans don't touch the metal railing, which looks as if it's harboring too many coats of paint.

"The colors are good, I'll give him that," she says surveying the dark red living room and the soft sage on the curved wall. She laughs. "These stairs are the same color as your bloody car!" At the top of the stairs is a half wall. The front side is living room red, top capped with maple colored plywood. The inside is covered in fabric. "Is this grass cloth?" Pauline runs the back of her hand across the wall. "Shit. This damn ring catches on everything."

"It's a string type paper."

She detaches a long thread, surveys the largest and warmest room in the house.

"Obviously the former owner once removed put that up." The paper is cream colored with dark blue, green, and blood red flecks in it. "Is there a bathroom up here?"

I point to the side of the room at the center of which is a six-foot wide section of wall containing a closet with mirrored bi-fold doors.

"Where the hell did he get those?"

"Impressive, aren't they. The bathroom is behind there. The doors are nine feet tall."

"My assistant will spend all day looking at herself and never get anything done," Pauline cackles.

She leans toward the mirrors and examines her nose; moves into the bathroom on the left side of the closet. "A claw foot tub! I could remove that and take it home! My sixteen year old would just die to have it!"

"The closet doors are from a home a previous owner has in Phoenix. The whole structure looks transparent from the outside. The locals call it the glass house."

"Okay. I want to buy, despite the fact there is no bathroom door," she says, emerging on the right side of the closet and leaning against the wall there. "This will be interesting. I can use it the way it is. My assistant can have the lower floor and I'll have the upper. The commode is right behind the closet. Not a problem for either of us. Why did the architect not do anything about the yard?"

"I believe he wanted to maintain a low profile."

"And the incomplete changes to the outside?"

"Complete and purposely done."

"Looks like an unfinished painting. Ah! Art imitating life on the outside of a home? Tacky."

She's already moving down the spiral and heading for the front door. The metal shakes. I follow reluctantly. Outside on the sidewalk Pauline studies the taupe stucco and black window frames which grace the front and half of the right side of the tall house.

I leave her, escape to the back and examine the flat clapboard profile that wraps to meet the stucco on one side and completely covers the other.

"Do you think the two exteriors are properly sealed where they join?"

Pauline bellows.

I walk toward her, resisting the urge to cover my ears with my hands.

"I mean how did they do that? Where are the furnace and the water heater?" Her voice reaches a higher pitch, makes me cringe.

"The house exterior was completed nine years ago and there are no signs of moisture damage on the inside walls," I say quietly. "The exterior is completely sealed. The furnace and water heater are in the recessed section of the closet by the back door."

"I hope you can give me the name of a repairman who is not claustrophobic! Alarm system?" she yells over her shoulder as she crosses the lawn to the other side of the house.

I climb four wooden steps and walk in Pauline's direction on the wrap-around black porch.

"Also in the back closet."

"Okay. Let's do supper and talk offers."

I watch the woman pace back and forth. "I'm not available for dinner."

She looks up at me, puzzled. "What?"

"And the price is fixed. The owner won't move at all."

"Fixed? No dinner? A fixed price? How do you make money? Look, I'm prepared to offer, say two hundred, and I'll write a cheque for half right now."

She follows me, stumbles on the uneven ground.

"Half is too much."

"What?"

"Good faith is demonstrated quite decently by ten percent; exceptionally by fifteen."

"What about the damn price," she yells from the bottom of the porch steps?

"I told you, it's fixed."

I go through the front door. Don't hold it open for the woman. It slams back toward the wall behind it.

"What the fuck is your game?" she says through her teeth.

"No game. Quite simple really. The price is the price."

I jog quickly up the spiral stairs and turn off the lights in the bathroom and bedroom. Pauline is blocking the way at the bottom. "Let me through. I need to lock the front door. We'll leave by the back after I set the alarm."

Pauline moves but I still have to brush up against her to pass. She keeps pace with me. "You've memorized the alarm code? Oh, I get it. Sleeping with the owner?"

"Every night."

"I knew it! When Andrew told me about you. I knew you couldn't possibly be genuine."

I move through the kitchen. She follows me, pulls the stainless oven door open and lets it slam back into place.

"Can you step outside please?" I ask.

"I want this property. I'll deal only with the owner. I want his name."

"Her."

"I want *her* name, then."

I stand on the bottom rung of the ladder, reach inside the closet, which begins to emit a series of short beeps. "Okay, we have approximately fifty-five seconds." I fold the ladder, tuck it in its original place, open the door, and step outside. The beeps are getting closer together. "Pauline—"

The woman moves slowly. A long piercing beep begins as I close the door. I swipe a plastic card through a rectangular box.

Pauline looks up. "Where's the lock box?" she asks.

"I don't need one," I say.

"How long are you planning to hold on to this house? What is it to you? A former lover's home?"

She follows me to the edge of the property, looks up and down the river. I walk towards the MG with Pauline in tow, look back at her when she stumbles trying to keep up. "I'm the owner."

"Come on, let's just sit down over supper. Let me invite my husband and we'll work this out. Between the two of us we can pay cash."

"The price is still fixed. Perhaps the two of you need to discuss that before we sit down together. Now, I really have to run, I'm hoping to rent a property in Montgomery and I hate to keep people waiting."

I stand next to the MG, change my shoes for runners, and pull a windbreaker over my dress. "Leave a message for me next week and I'll let you know if the place is still available."

I slam the door and turn the ignition key. Pauline looks furious and amazed. I rev the motor a few times, depress the clutch, and drive off. I imagine the heave of her substantial chest under her crossed arms.

Chapter VII

Bertha is animated when I arrive for the interment.

"Here she is! How did the Inglewood sale go last week? Are you up or down? Jane! Reed! Marlo's here. Where are they? Did you see her new car? Everybody, this is Marlo. Ed's one and only child."

"I think they know that, *Mum*. Hi all—did I miss the food?"

"Funny aren't you. Let me see what you're wearing under that Macintosh. You're the only young person I know that owns one."

"It's Ed's."

"That's about as funny as you saying you're going to eat!" She peels the coat away to reveal a red knit dress. Fitted. Straight neckline. No sleeves. "I should have known," she says.

"What did you expect, black?" The front door, still slightly ajar, opens wider and Nemit comes in.

"Bloody hell," says Bertha.

"No kidding Mrs. G. The rain is something else."

Bertha glares at me. "Should I expect anyone else? Where's your son?"

"Ball practice."

"In this sort of weather?"

"They're inside. Catching. Did we miss the food?" Nemit asks.

"*We* did not," Bertha says. "I'll give you sixty-five dollars if you can get my daughter to eat anything on that table."

"Odd amount isn't it, *Mum*?"

"A dollar for every year of Ed's life," she says.

I slip my arm through Nemit's and we march downstairs to where Bertha has laid out a buffet of Ed's favorite breakfast food.

"Hello Victoria," I say to Bertha's neighbor. "You're looking well."

"Thank you dear, but life in a wheelchair just gets to be too much some days. As soon as my son tries to move me to that home he's been talking about I'm going to unpack my husband's gun and BANG."

"Don't you pay her any never mind, Marlo; she's getting a bit thick in her old age," Betty whispers to me.

"What did you say, Betty?" Nemit asks.

"I said she's getting a bit thick, dear, you know," her voice drops, "senile."

"I'd feel the same if my son wanted to lock me away somewhere," Nemit says, crouching so she's eye-level with Victoria. "I'd want to blow his silly head off. Have you had a bite to eat, Victoria?"

"Now, you're not Marlo, are you?"

"Nemit."

"Well, I would like a potato scone or two, I see them next to the strawberry preserves, and a bit of trifle too if you don't mind."

"Of course not. What about the fried bread, eggs, or ham and pineapple?"

Victoria lowers her voice, "Terrible when it's cold, and I've never known Bertha to have the talent to serve anything warm. Maybe a bap as well. That's lovely, thank you."

"How is Stan?" I ask Betty.

"Oh, he's wonderful, he is. Never could imagine myself with any other, dear. I'm a one-man woman I am. Don't have an understanding of the divorce craze at all. But maybe you can explain that to me one day. Another day," she says, taking in my dress. "Here's Stan now. I just sent him over the back for the big urn—over here Stan," she calls, as he comes in from the ground level patio.

"Well that's the wrong one! I said the forty-cup, not the twelve, dear. Excuse me Marlo, I must go, but you make sure you talk to me after. Stan, I just don't know how you could mis—" As her voice trails away Bertha motions me over to a group standing in a circle.

"Marlo, these are the people in my Tai-Chi classes. Mary-Anne from the Tuesday group. Deborah and Flora from the Wednesday, Roger, Bob, Kenneth and Veronica from Thursday—"

"The noon class?" I recognize some of the names.

"The noon class. Bill, Aileen, Walter and May, Andrew and Julie, Allan, and Shug—"

"Shug?"

"Hugh, honey. From Friday, and of course, your aunt Jane."

"Where are the Monday people?" I ask.

"Oh, we're all there on a Monday but not all together on the other days," says Bill. "We're all getting a wee bit older, you know."

Bertha moves away and I watch her go up the stairs to the kitchen.

"Now don't depress the girl, Bill," May says. "Especially no' the day."

"Do you have to be Scottish to take these particular classes?" I joke. There's a titter of laughter and Mary-Anne, a woman dressed in a bright sarong topped off with a white shirt tied at the waist, speaks up.

"I'm Canadian. The one and only!" Her multitude of silver bangles sound like chimes.

"I'm very pleased to meet you all. Did you know Ed well?"

"Oh, none of us ever met your father," Bill says. "We're just here to give your Mam a bit of support. That's what we do the best."

"Well I'm sure Bertha appreciates that. I'd better see if she needs help with anything." The circle closes in on the space I leave.

I see Reed across the room. Move towards him, arms out.

"How the hell are you?" he asks, hugging me a bit too close.

"I'm fine," I say, my voice muffled against his shoulder. "You can let me go now." One heavy arm stays around my neck.

"Sad day," he says.

"Not really."

"You're burying your Dad." His free hand suddenly covers his mouth. "I always thought you adored Ed."

"That's why I'm not sad. I mean I miss him. But—"

"But?"

"It's a long story."

"I know! Mum's been e-mailing me. Telling me the details. You know that generation is a lot happier if you just give in to their bents! You're dressed u—up," he sings. "Where are we going after?"

"I'm meeting Jack."

"Jac-tit-ation? The restless man behind the lens? Jane tells me all."

"Jesus Christ. Bertha too I hear. It's just business."

"She must be really pissed at you!"

Reed recognizes my indignant look.

"I'm going upstairs."

"Take it easy on her!" he calls.

The door chimes sound. Bertha emerges at the top of the staircase.

"Okay everyone! Can I have your attention? The cars are here." Betty and Stan re-appear at the patio door. He's carrying the right urn. "Just set that on the table if you would for now, Stan," Bertha says, "and can you manage Victoria round to the Handi-Bus?"

"Never you mind love. I'll manage that fine, I will," Stan says.

"I'll come too darling; hold the brolly over us and over the old dear," Betty adds.

"I'm not an old dear, Betty. I hear every word you say. Every word!"

"Okay Vic-toria, not to worry, Stan here is a wonderful driver, aren't you Stan?"

"Marlo, could you lock that door after them, please?" Bertha asks.

"I'll get it, Bertha," Nemit hollers.

"Well, could she unplug the warming plates as well then?" Bertha asks me.

"I'm on it, Bertha," Nemit calls back. "Marlo, I'll be up in a minute."

The Tai-Chi group fills the stairs.

"Are we in the second car then?" Bill asks.

"The second car," Bertha says quietly.

"Do you have the urn, Bertha?" I ask.

"The urn?"

"The reason all Ed's best friends are here today."

Bertha disappears down the hall. Jane turns to me. "Do you have to be this sarcastic all the time?" she asks. Then she follows her sister.

"It's the stress," Nemit says, from the top step. "Come on. Put your shoes on. Get the Mac. I'm going out. Looks like they're a bit confused."

I slip on a pair of red sling-back shoes with narrow heels. "I'm coming," I say. I hold the Macintosh over my head. "Get under here!" I say to Nemit. "All right! Those of you who won't fit in the second limousine, please join Victoria, Betty and Stan in the Handi-Bus."

"Can I go in there too?" Nemit asks.

"I was hoping you'd come in the first car with Bertha, Jane, Reed and me."

"Please?"

"Mary-Anne?"

"Victoria," she says.

"I should have known."

I nod to the driver, who is gallantly holding a golf umbrella over his own head. I signal toward the doorway where Jane is locking up and Bertha is bent in a cramp-like embrace around the urn.

"Your shoes," Bertha says, as she walks past me to the waiting car.

"Ruined already," Reed laughs. When they settle inside the car he adds, "What color was the pair you wore the last time you were out there?"

"Do you have to be this much of an asshole all the time?" I ask.

"It's the stress," Nemit repeats, getting in and sitting close to me.

"Remember the last chauffeured trip we made together?" Bertha asks, tearfully rubbing the urn.

"You mean over to England?" I ask, as the car pulls around the island in the middle of the crescent.

"Up to the pass," Bertha says, sobbing.

I sink back, watch the second car and the Handi-Bus circle after us.

"You with us, Marlo?" Jane's voice penetrates the confines of the long white car. "It's okay Bertha," she continues. "I told you it wouldn't be any easier if you waited."

"I was thinking about the chopper ride."

"Seven years since Joel," Nemit says.

"Ten," I reply.

"Ed loved that man," Bertha sits back, perching the urn on the edge of her lap.

The three vehicles reach the cemetery fifteen minutes later. A formally dressed crowd is gathered under a square awning and four men in tails move their feet restlessly on the fringe.

"Are they musicians?" Bertha asks.

"My God! One of them has a tambourine!" says Jane.

"I could have played the pipes if you'd asked me to, auntie," Reed offers.

"Imagine the pipes out here," Jane says. "Absolutely majestic in the shadow of those mountains," she continues, sniffling. The car stops. The Tai Chi group emerges, umbrellas up. They gather about the Handi-Bus.

"I'll go help them," Nemit says, opening the door.

She joins the group, watches the electric ramp lower Victoria to ground level and holds her umbrella over the woman.

"Well, that wasn't at all a bad drive," Betty says. "I said not bad—was it Victoria?"

"I'm not deaf, you clown."

"Well I never! Stan—Stan? Stanley where are you?" Stan stands next to Mary-Anne. The rain makes her sarong cling to her legs.

The driver of the second car motions the group toward a small hole in the ground. Its edges are draped with bright green indoor-outdoor carpeting.

"How was your drive in the limousine, Reed?" Betty asks, squeezing between Reed and her husband.

"A lot more comfortable than the bloody bus, I'll bet," Stan says, while the group stares.

"Make room for the family, please."

Jane is still in the car with Bertha and me.

"Here," Bertha says to me. "I think you should carry."

She plunks the urn on my lap. My hands automatically reach and balance but I'm not prepared for the weight. The lid bounces on the rubber-covered flooring. I thought burial urns were sealed. I watch Bertha take her sister's hand and step out of the car.

"When you're ready," the driver says to me through the open door.

I place the urn carefully on the floor and reach for the lid. "A moment please."

He bends and lifts the round lid, stares inside the urn for a wide-eyed moment and gently replaces it.

"Well, Ed," I say. "I guess you really are gone."

Och naw, echoes about me.

"You don't have a voice," I say. "You're dead."

The driver coughs in front of the car door and my gaze meets Jane's.

Just think of me as a wee annoyance, pet.

Kind of like Jane? I think.

Kinda like Jane.

I pull the Macintosh around me and wrap the urn in a gray cocoon. The driver holds an umbrella over my head and stumbles with me towards the huddled group.

"Mum," I say at the edge of the tiny hole in the ground, "Mum, where's the priest?"

"What priest?"

"The one who usually says the prayers for the dead. The one who usually sprinkles the coffin with holy water."

"There's no coffin, dear. Your red shoes are going to be ruined."

"Let me take that for you now," the driver says to me, motions with the umbrella handle.

Bill starts to hum "Amazing Grace."

"No, I'll do it," I reply.

I kneel awkwardly, legs covered by the Mac. I lower the urn into the square. Bertha doesn't make a sound. I stand and begin the "Our Father."

"Which art in heaven," the group continues. Throughout the prayer Betty's voice is the loudest.

"And deliver us from evil, Amen," signals the end.

"Would anyone like to say something about Ed?" I ask. "Mum?"

Bertha stares at the ground in front of my red shoes.

"Mum?" I ask again.

"This is not really a good-bye," she begins. "Ed is simply—simply—" she doesn't finish.

"You've got to let go of him, love," Betty says. "You said to my Stan that this was about moving on, didn't she Stan? And now here in the presence of all these people you can."

A large procession enters the cemetery. Bertha looks past the group and watches a white hearse snake forward. Cars follow, circle the main drive, and coil around the Garden of Remembrance. The last few vehicles park near the Handi-Bus. Their passengers walk-run toward the bigger group.

"I wonder who that is?" Betty says.

"Ready, Bertha?" I ask.

She moves away from Jane, reaches down, takes a handful of wet earth and drops it into the opening. Once she's seated inside the car the rest of the group does the same.

Nemit helps Stan maneuver Victoria close to the opening. She bends and fills the older woman's hand. Another hearse glides toward us.

"Thank you dear," Victoria says to Nemit. "What are you doing for dinner?"

Chapter VIII

I meet Jack for dinner. Nothing elaborate. I choose a small bistro in Kensington. He has worked with a lawyer. Intends to sue me for half of the value of my properties: the house I live in, the house in Inglewood, the two original apartments, the two four-plexes, and the cabin which is inside the holding company while the woman who owns it finalizes her divorce. The cabin title is registered to a male, a mister Findley, a Trojan, the sort you can't trace in the Alberta registry database—unless you are a vet.

"Not going to happen," I say, over a plate of ziti.

"When did you start eating cheese?" Jack asks.

"When I was a wee girl," I reply.

He drinks bottled water and eats greens. No dressing, no tomatoes, no bread. I hand him another copy of the prenuptial agreement he signed before I married him in eighty-nine.

"The rules have changed," he says. "Either partner can sue for more alimony when they are under duress."

"Maintenance. You and I never agreed to pay each other anything."

"I think we should."

"You are wasting your time," I say. "Eight and a half years—clearly you've over-estimated the Alberta Statute of Limitations."

He leaves five minutes later, unsatisfied. I stay and enjoy my meal, pay the bill, drive home. Only then do I allow myself to wonder if he'll succeed. I remember the Alberta woman, Irene Murdoch, who got almost nothing after breaking her back on the family farm for twenty-five years. A judicial decision took her lifeblood away.

Have you ever noticed how your partner can cut you to the quick? Assault the very piece of you that you think you guard best? *The greatest defence is an offence.* Ed teaches me that when we play soldier with Reed. Wives should plant thick groves, dig moats, prepare for late attacks.

Chapter IX

"How was the rest of your night?" Nemit asks, the next day.

"How was the rest of your night?" I ask.

"Fantastic! Victoria is a gourmet."

"NmmHmm."

"You don't sound very enthusiastic. Tired?" she asks.

"Nnn—ope."

"I am."

"The water's encroaching on the path behind the garage," I say.

"What do you mean encroaching? Don't change the subject."

"Jack is cold."

"You needed someone to confirm that for you? You okay?"

"No. He wants to sue me."

"Want me to come over?"

"No. I mean it. There's water four feet from the garage."

"What did the enviro-man say? I'm coming over right after I pick up Adam."

As soon as I hang up, the doorbell rings. I wait a few minutes and it rings again. I hear Bertha's muted voice interspersed by her palm style knock on the door.

"I'm coming!" I yell.

"It's about time! How come you're not dressed for church?"

"I'm not well."

"Not well?"

"Not well."

"You know I hate going alone. What's wrong with you?"

"I don't know."

"You don't know?"

"I don't know, Bertha. Listen, I have to—organize. I don't think I'll go today."

Bertha looks at me as she sinks into the overstuffed sofa. "Don't sit down," she says. "Take a shower. Maybe you'll feel better and we can make the noon mass instead of the ten-thirty."

"Give me a minute, okay."

"So what did you think of the group yesterday?"

"The Monday Tuesday Wednesday Friday bunch? Not bad."

Bertha sits up straight and smoothes her polyester pants. I imagine the moisture they siphon out of her skin.

"Mary-Anne is a hoot. How old is she?"

"Seventy-nine."

"You're kidding. I thought she was less than sixty."

"That's what ten years of unobstructed chi does for you."

"What?"

"That's how long she and her husband have been going to Tai Chi. That's where they met. She wants to know the name of Jack's business. Wants to have some photos done."

"Photos? Good God!"

"Obsession is not exclusively for the young. How about that shower? I'll make you something while you're upstairs."

"I'm not really hungry."

"You wearing anything under that skimpy robe?"

"There's no-one else here, Bertha."

A white car pulls up on the driveway.

"Who the heck is that now? Jesus, Mary, and Joseph," Bertha says, squinting through the wood blinds. "It's Nemit."

"She is worried about me."

"I'll just bet she is. Do up your belt. The boy is with her. Do you know where *she* stayed last night? That woman—"

"Back off, okay. Victoria invited her."

Bertha sucks in her breath and crosses her arms. I open the door.

"Hi Marlo!"

"Hi Adam. Where were you last night?"

"At my buddy Jason's. He has everything. A pool table, a big screen TV."

"Yes, but does he have—?" I tease.

"Don't say it!" Adam looks at Nemit—

"A urinal?" Nemit and I say together.

"You have a urinal in your home?" Bertha asks Nemit.

"Yep. Had to have one bastion of male paraphernalia for Adam!"

"Jesus Christ," Bertha says.

"Mrs. Gilman! My mom doesn't like that kind of language, especially on holy days. I'm starving."

"Sorry. I was just about to cook something."

"Can I watch?" Adam asks.

"You can help me," Bertha replies. "Come on." Adam follows her to the kitchen.

"Do you mind being stuck with Mum for a bit while I shower?"

"No. I'll amuse myself, but now that I've met Victoria I won't have to for quite a while."

"You are bad. I thought when you had those photos done for Joy that—"

"That what?"

"That she had come back for good."

"She didn't."

"I'll be down in about twenty minutes. Don't let her cook anything for me."

"Okay, I'll try not to look like I'm supervising."

When Nemit enters the kitchen Adam hums over some scrambled eggs. "Where's Bertha?"

"In the garage."

"Don't let them stick." Nemit goes out through the patio doors and mumbles, "She was right." Water seeps through three-quarters of the lawn and a puddle grows a few feet from the garage. The side door is open and Nemit can see Bertha's stocking feet doing a balancing act on the workbench. Her upper body is out of sight, but it's clear that she's reaching for something.

"Mum! Tell Mrs. Gilman that the eggs are ready."

"Okay, Adam," Nemit says.

"I'll be right in," Bertha calls from the garage.

The woman has the ears of a bat, Nemit thinks. She watches Bertha put something in her pocket and goes inside.

"Can I eat these? Mrs. Gilman says Marlo takes forever to get ready. Can I, Mom?"

"Go ahead."

"Think Marlo will mind if I go in the den?"

"I don't think so."

110

"Coffee, Bertha?" Nemit asks.

"Sure Nemit. Do you know how to make that?"

Adam snickers. Eggs spurt through his lips. "My Mom makes me some every morning before school."

"You feed your son coffee?"

Adam swallows the last of the eggs and toast. "Can I go now, Mum?"

Bertha ruffles his thick brown hair. "Gotcha!" she says.

"And don't touch anything!" Nemit calls as he bolts up the stairs two at a time.

"Can I try on Lynn's old camo vest?" he asks me half way up.

"I like the look of you two in my kitchen," I say to Nemit and my mother. They both scowl.

"Church?" Bertha points at her watch.

"But Nemit and Adam are here," I say.

"I'd love to come with you today," Nemit says. "Adam likes to go to Catholic Church. All that off-key singing and the glitzy outfits the priests wear, he's right into it."

"I never thought of sacramental robes as glitz—y," Bertha says.

"Oops—did I hit a nerve?" Nemit asks. "What are you hiding in Marlo's garage? Chocolate?"

"What?" I say. "You're hiding something in the garage?"

"Just checking for the sponge brush to edge with," she says. "The bathroom? Remember?"

Nemit stares at the bulge in Bertha's blazer pocket. Re-fills the coffee cups.

"Mrs. G...there's dust or something on your blazer and on the floor," Adam says. "Can I have more juice? Can I take it upstairs?"

Bertha hurries toward the bathroom.

"Bertha!" I call. "It's almost time to go!" There's no answer. "Are you coming?"

She emerges a few minutes later, face flushed.

"Are we going in your car?" Adam asks.

"Saints preserve us!" Bertha says, clamping her hand over her mouth.

Adam is wrapped in the red and gold-edged sari I wore when I married Raj. There's a lipstick dot in the middle of his forehead and he's wearing the beaded sling-backs that Bertha adores.

"Th—the shoes," she blurts.

"I know, but Marlo got the red ones wet."

≋≋≋

After I park the Rover, I find Bertha in the soundproof, glass-fronted crèche at the back of St. Bernard's. "Why are we in this ridiculous room?" I ask.

"Because we are late and because there isn't a seat to be had anywhere," she says.

"I love babies!" Adam says to Bertha. He coos at a child trying to worm out of its father's arms.

"It's noisy and we can't see anything," Bertha says.

"Well, I gave you the option of not coming." Bertha's cold hard stare doesn't rattle me. "It's a game," I say to Nemit. "The guilt game. We play it weekly—ever since Ed died."

Bertha kneels behind a couple trying to manage one-year-old twin girls. She bends her head over her clasped hands.

"What do you think she's praying for?" Nemit asks.

"She usually tells me after mass is over. Could be anything—something on sale that she walked by, or you."

Bertha turns around and motions us to join her.

"We don't have to whisper in here, Mum," I say. "We're surrounded by soundproof glass. Look—there's the woman who sat in front of us a couple of weeks ago."

"Where?"

"Third pew from the back. I bet she comes to the noon mass so that she doesn't have to put up with us!"

"That's hilarious," Nemit says. "I'll sit over here. Looks like some baby stuff there, Marlo. Watch your cape."

"Shit."

"Oh, I'm so sorry," says twins' mother. "Here, let me get that."

The woman produces a moistened cloth from a bag covered in blue and pink teddies. She dries the seat with a clean diaper and Nemit sits down.

"Please stand for the Gospel reading," comes over the speaker.

We stand. Bertha and I make small signs of the cross on our foreheads, lips and chest.

"Why do they do that?" Adam asks.

"Something to do with the crucifixion," Nemit says to him, then she puts her arm around Adam's waist and they make faces at the twins.

"Mom, can I have a baby something?"

"No," Nemit replies.

"But I get lonely."

"So do I when you're not around, bud, but just imagine—" The twin nearest them throws a plastic bottle at the glass and begins crying. "The mess."

The twins convince their parents to leave. Bertha immediately takes over the front row of seats next to the glass. "This is so much better!" she says to me.

"Come," she pats the seat next to her. "Why was that boy wearing one of your dresses?" she whispers.

"He has good taste, doesn't he? He was wearing my favourite."

"You told me you don't have a favourite."

"I lied."

"So Raj was your favourite husband?"

"No."

"Mine was Joel," she says.

"Here we go!" I say, looking back at Nemit and Adam. "Get up here!" I mouth to Nemit.

"Ed loved that man."

"Like his own son—I know, Mum. Let's talk about Ed."

"Ed?"

"The man we buried yesterday."

"We didn't bury Ed yesterday," Bertha whimpers, "he's right here." She places a hand over her heart.

"Can I stand on the kneeling thing so I can see better? Mom?"

"Okay, but take your shoes off first," Nemit says. "O God, Bertha, are you okay?" She hands Bertha the dry diaper that the twins left behind. Bertha dabs at her eyes. "I found the sermon particularly moving as well," Nemit says. "Had nothing to do with the gospel story of the prodigal son but the priest really had me going with that stuff about father-son relationships. I almost wish that Adam had one!"

Bertha folds the diaper neatly and hands it back. "Do you not think he's missing something, dear?" she asks Nemit.

"Bertha, don't," I say.

"I mean a boy needs more than a urinal."

"Mum, that's enough!"

"Well it's true!"

"Mrs. G," Adam says, "I like my urinal. All my friends think it's cool."

"Right now I'd guess I'm a lot happier than either of you two," Nemit says.

I stare at my friend.

"I mean the two of you don't know how to communicate with each other. You pussyfoot around and don't talk about what you need to talk about."

"Mom, the man in the back is staring at you," Adam says.

"I don't care, Adam." She turns back to us. "One of you is mooning over a man that no one else liked," Bertha sucks in her breath, "and the other collects husbands for a living."

"What?" I say, in disbelief.

"You go around grasping at scarecrows and worse, marrying them."

"That's enough, dear," Bertha says. "We are in church."

"Don't give me that bullshit."

"Mom—it's Sunday," Adam hisses.

The man at the back leaves the room, arms around his small child.

"What's gotten into you?" I ask.

"You talk about the games Bertha plays, well what about you?" Nemit asks.

"What about me?"

"She must be jealous, dear," Bertha adds.

"What?" Nemit explodes.

"Of Marlo, here." Bertha puts her arm around my shoulder.

An usher enters the room with the collection basket. "Ladies?"

"No thank you," I say.

"Everything all right in here?"

"Fine!" Adam says.

The usher gestures toward the glass. We look out and meet the glares of the people returning from the altar.

"I've missed communion?" Bertha whines.

"It's not a big deal, Mum."

Bertha pushes past Nemit and me. Outside the door she buttons her blazer and pulls it down by the bottom edge. Holding her head up, she walks toward a line of people moving slowly toward the priest.

"Ed was right," Nemit says to me.

"About what?" I say.

"About Joel."

≈≈≈

After mass, Bertha and Adam go inside the house. Nemit and I walk shoeless across the wet grass to my property line.

"Why is the water warm?" she asks me.

"Don't know," I reply.

"Strange, no?"

"Yes."

"Stranger that your mother sneaks in and out of your garage, no?" she says gently.

"Maybe," I say. When Nemit and I go inside we hear Bertha and Adam laughing.

"They must be upstairs," Nemit says.

"Mother of God!"

Bertha wears a long off-white shift, jangles fifteen gold bracelets and finger-waves a plain gold band at Nemit and me. Her clothes and Adam's clothes are hanging from the wardrobe door.

"You're wearing the wrong jewellery," I say seriously.

"I got the rest right, though—right?" Bertha replies.

Nemit stares at Bertha's bare feet. "Yep," she says. "No shoes that time."

"The shift is too long for you Mum," I say, surprised to discover that I don't want her to walk on the hem.

Bertha looks at me sideways. "This afternoon, Adam is wearing Victorian lace," she says in her best London accent. "The dress contrasts sharply with the ruby ring, and complements the square-toed slipp-ahs and the plain-Jane veil."

"I don't really like this dress," Adam says. "The inside is really scratchy."

"You and I need to get home," Nemit says. She stares at me, raises her eyebrows.

"But I want to see you in one!" Adam whines.

"I'm too big for Marlo's clothes," Nemit replies.

"Not the sari," he says.

I shake my head in disbelief. I'll never get over the attraction people have to bridal regalia, especially *my* bridal regalia.

"Please? Please? Mom? Put it on!" Adam says.

"I'll get you the *right* jewellery," Bertha says, wriggling her hand out of the bracelets. "Come on!"

"That leaves the gown for me," I say, moving to the wardrobe.

Bertha hands the folded lengths of the sari to Nemit, who slips off the long cotton skirt and matching sweater that she wore to mass.

"Well?" Nemit says to me. "Don't tell me that you're feeling nostalgic!"

"Very funny," I say, slipping on the gown Thomas bought for me.

Adam helps Nemit. He circles around his mother, who raises one arm in the air.

"Try not to step on the dress Adam!" Bertha says. "Let me do up the hooks for you dear," she says, turning to me. "Oh, they won't close—you've—never mind. The scarf," she says, draping it across my shoulders. "The shoes."

I slip them on.

"Shall we eat?" Bertha extends her hand.

"Let's!" Adam takes it.

They lead our mock parade down the stairs and into the kitchen. While Bertha, Nemit and Adam fuss with the table, I disappear outside.

I know that Bertha's on her toes, peering out over the kitchen sink. After a few minutes of struggling to get the canoe down, I raise the electric door. I know that Bertha hears the small motor and brushes off the noise, but I also know that the sound of Styrofoam scraping against damp cement will be more than she can stand.

When I round the corner from the garage the trio steps out onto the deck and stares. I've pulled the train through my legs and tucked it into the too small bodice of my strapless dress. There's a great wad of fabric between my legs. The skirted layers of netting and taffeta look like a puffy diaper.

"That's right, cover up those ridiculous things that masquerade as underwear," Bertha says, stretching her neck from side to side. "Thongs cut off the circulation to the clitoris you know," she says to Nemit.

"Oh, I know," Nemit replies.

"Don't just stand there! Help me!" I say.

"Help you?" Nemit asks.

"Help me," I repeat.

Adam is the only one who reacts. He steps out of the Victorian lace gown and gently lays it over Bertha's arm. He moves to the stern of the yellow canoe that I drag toward the waterlogged lawn. His boxers fill with air. The veil he wears balloons behind his head.

"I don't get it," Nemit paces on the deck. "What the heck are you doing?"

"What does it look like?" I ask.

Then I notice Bertha. She stares at Nemit, seems to admire the sari as it brushes the top of her feet. The end of the sari tries to jump forward over Nemit's shoulder. Bertha catches it and tucks it in.

"The two of you are such a pair," Nemit continues.

"Of *what*?" I ask, setting the canoe down and straightening up.

"Ow!" Adam says after leaning his scrawny thigh into the stationary boat.

"Of—of—dysfunctional misfits!" she says.

"And you are different from us how?" I ask, cocking my head to one side. "Aren't we all disguised?"

"What are we doing with the canoe, dear?" Bertha asks. "If you are planning an excursion, then it'll have to wait until after we eat."

I lift the canoe front and kick the Styrofoam support away from the hull. Adam tries to do the same at the other end, but he's too short. Lifting is all he can manage. Nemit pulls the other block out.

"I'm not sure how you plan to fit all four of us in there," Bertha says.

"Four of us can't go in one canoe," Adam adds.

"All right, I'll stay back and the three of you can go, although I don't know how you think I can pick you up now that you're driving that tiny car, Marlo, and I am not—definitely not, letting you put that thing on top of the Rover."

"We're not paddling today," I say. "Let's go in and eat."

Nemit continues to stare at the canoe resting in the soggy grass. "What next? Waiting for *the flood*?"

"You're really plucky when you're having sex," I shoot back.

"Just talk to your mother."

"No one can *just talk* to Bertha."

"Try," she says.

When we sit at the table, Adam back in the dress and my legs covered again, Bertha sets out the food. Nemit looks back and forth between my mother and me. We both pretend to ignore her.

"Adam, would you like to say grace?" Bertha asks.

"Okay—" he clears his throat. "Lord—sustain our bodies with this food, our hearts with true friendship and our mothers with—" he giggles at me.

"With what?" Nemit asks impatiently.

"Understanding," he says.

"And?" Nemit continues.

"The end?" he says.

"Amen." Bertha says. "Very nice, dear. Where did you learn that one? From your mom?"

"At Jason's house," he says.

"What church do they go to?" I ask.

"A united something of something," he says. "Can I eat now?"

We're quiet except for the sound of Adam's legs swinging inside the lace-covered dress.

"Yes, you can eat now," I say chin down, staring at the gap between my chest and the bodice of my old wedding dress.

"Where's the other dress?" Nemit asks.

"The other dress?"

"The dress you wore when you married Joel?"

"I got rid of it a long time ago."

"Got rid of it?"

"Got rid of it—Why do I always have to repeat myself for you two?"

"I don't believe you," Bertha says. "You can't let go of the house the two of you lived in. Where is it?"

"Inglewood."

"Not the house, the dress," Nemit says. "We want to know."

"I showed the house last week," I say to Bertha.

"And when do you expect to close?" she asks.

"Don't have the right buyer yet."

"How many years has it been empty now?" Nemit asks. "Ten?"

"How can there possibly be a right one?" Bertha joins in. "You're selling a piece of real estate."

"Not exactly," I say.

"Of course exactly. What is wrong with this buyer? Are you worried about the neighbours? Did they want to change the place? What?" Bertha asks.

"Where is the dress?" Nemit asks again.

"I know what's coming next, Bertha, but please, don't talk to me about not letting go."

"Why not?" she and Nemit say together.

My hands shake, even although I rest them on the table.

"I let go of plenty," Bertha says.

"That's your cue!" Nemit adds.

"All right! Mum? Can I watch TV?" Adam asks.

"No. Time to get dressed," Nemit whispers. She and Adam leave the table.

"Let go? Plenty of what?" I say, voice rising.

"That den is full of leftover stuff from five husbands!" Bertha starts. "Piles of goodies—from tents to rings to empty shells to expired birth control pills!"

"Yes, but the men are gone," I say.

"I've let go—you're the one that still keeps Ed's stuff in the garage! His tool belt, his coveralls, his work boots—this whole place is a museum."

I stand as the front door closes.

"You're not eating your quiche," Bertha yells. I move to the pantry. "What? Going to make one of those ridiculous shakes again?"

I retrieve a brown paper grocery bag.

"Oh, what now?" she asks. "A surprise?"

I place the bag on the counter top and reach my hand inside. The edge slices into to the soft flesh of my upper arm.

"Shit!" I say.

"Figures," Bertha says. "You were *so* clumsy as a child!"

I hold two small plastic bags over my head. Bertha covers her face with her hands. "Explain, Mum!"

"Let me get some peroxide for that cut."

"No!"

"I mean it—you don't know where that paper bag's been." Bertha gets up and rifles through the cupboards.

"You leave me at Edenbrook!" I yell. "You give a reception for people Ed didn't ever know! You insist on the procession to the graveyard—you *make* me carry an urn!"

"No one *makes* you do anything!"

"I don't get it, Bertha," I say, fighting for control.

"Come here, darling, I'll try to explain."

I move toward my mother, arms outstretched. Bertha dabs a cotton ball soaked in peroxide on my arm. "Ow!"

"Don't be such a baby."

I take the cotton and throw it in the sink. Bertha lifts the bottle of peroxide but I take it from her hand and throw it as well. She still says nothing. Peroxide fizzes in the sink. I wrap my arms around my mother and stroke her head.

"It's normal to miss him," I say. "It's normal to hold on. But to hold a fake burial?" I hold Bertha at arm's length. "The whole thing is a sham! What is the point?"

"We started on a journey together—and it's not over."

"Dad is dead."

"He's just in a different place."

I pick up the bags again. "What's this? Man-in-a-sack? Dad-in-a-bag?" I hold the bags over the floor, my hands moving rapidly together and apart as I speak.

"BE careful!" Bertha says, arms out front, fingers splayed. She moves toward the brown bag on the counter, picks it up, embraces it.

"What are you planning to do with these remains?" I ask. I throw the bags up in the air and catch them again.

"Marlo!"

"Now I know why there was no priest yesterday—even you can't lie to one." My hands grip the bags and the contents bulge around my fingers.

"Watch it!" Bertha yells. "You'll burst them!"

"Why couldn't you just have kept the urn?" I pace. "Why couldn't we have forgone the whole ceremonial charade? I don't understand you!" *Easy lassie*, echoes in my head. I toss the baggies into the paper bag.

Still cradling the brown bag, Bertha lifts her purse off the couch in the living room and walks toward the front door.

"Oh, no, you don't!" I grab Bertha's arm. "You are *not* leaving until we figure something out!" The bag rustles as Bertha tightens her grip and shrugs me off. Suddenly I'm fifteen, but she's me and I'm her. "Mum. Mum," I say gently. "Sit down here, okay?"

"Why did you drag out the canoe?"

"Because I think we should take a trip."

"Another trip?"

"Another trip. On the Bow."

"I'm not fooled, Marlo."

"Mum, he has to go. You have to let him be."

"I have let him be. Look here." She pulls out a bag of ashes and it rocks, suspended from her fist. "Here he is. He can be whatever he wants."

"He's contained."

"Oh, you're brilliant. Finally you understand. It's the same way he kept me all those years."

"Mum."

"I loved the man. I only tried to leave him once, remember that?" She's crying now. "I did everything for him, everything."

"I know."

"And he still—" She gasps for air, hyperventilates, gathers the brown bag around her nose and mouth.

"But none of that makes any sense, Bertha. Then why don't you want him out of your life?"

"I—love—him. Don't you get it? Don't—you—understand? Love transcends all."

"Mum, sometimes *love* has nothing to do with why couples stay together."

"Don't, Marlo!" She crushes the brown paper bag to her chest.

"I've been married five times. It's not love that keeps couples together, it's their belief system or their fear of being alone, or their finances or a thousand other reasons that have nothing to do with *love*."

"No!"

"Dad wasn't always good to you."

"I'm his widow." She starts sobbing again, tears staining taffeta.

I stroke her thick short hair. "You're distraught. The Bow, let's take Ed with us."

"Let him go—in the river?"

"Look outside, behind my house. Since you left Ed in the garage the water keeps rising. None of my neighbours have seepage problems."

"And the whirlpool at my place. When?" Bertha asks.

"Soon," I reply.

Chapter X

"Have you ever wondered why women can't fish?" I ask Bertha.

"What do you mean? Of course women can fish," she replies.

"But have you ever wondered why they always throw the catch back in the river?" I continue.

"No—" she says, "and I think you are generalizing."

We stand on an outcrop of rock overlooking the headwaters of the Bow River. Nemit and Adam throw pebbles into the liquid pillow covering a boulder downstream.

"How far below the surface?" Nemit asks Adam.

"I can't tell Mom. I can't hear rock hitting rock. Can you?"

"No—look for a bigger stone."

Bertha holds a small baggie of ashes. The top is open and the air currents above the river draw the lighter contents toward the noisy flow. After two minutes Bertha chokes the top closed. I expect her to cry, but the only moisture on her face comes from the air.

"Your turn," she says.

I Frisbee my least favourite headdress into the headwaters, conservationists be damned. The throw involves my whole body, as if the headpiece has weight.

"Careful!" Bertha says. "Don't fall in!" The water envelops what I surrender.

"One," I say.

"One," she repeats.

We watch the tiara-style headpiece float downstream. Adam yells to Nemit and points.

"I thought it would sink immediately," Bertha says, laughing.

"Plastic underneath. Swiss lace. Nineteen seventy-seven." I jump boulder to boulder, fascinated.

"I thought it was wire," Bertha continues.

"Nope," I say, arms out for balance.

The material separates from the plastic cutout. The glue, brittle with age, dissolves immediately. Embroidered daisies bob. Adam runs along the hollow-sounding dirt bank below me.

"Aw—the daisies are sinking!" he cries.

The plastic is vacuumed into a sieve-like strain and drowns in a logjam.

"Adam! Adam!" Nemit screams. He's prone. Hangs over the bank from the waist up.

"I can see it Mummy!" He jumps to his feet. "Marlo, can I use your fishing rod?" The headpiece hangs on a submerged branch. "Look," he says, pointing. "We can't leave it there."

"All right," I say to him.

He runs to the car.

"He can try," I say, to Nemit's disapproving stare. "It's not likely that he'll hook it."

"It's moving again!" Bertha says.

When I look back the headpiece floats free under the surface. We watch as the plastic shape gains speed, plunges over a two-meter ledge, and disappears in the souse hole.

Adam comes back, bounces my fishing rod in front of him, stands feet apart next to Bertha.

"Gone?" he asks Bertha.

"Gone," she replies.

"Why doesn't it come out?" Adam asks me.

"A couple of reasons," I say. "The water might have flipped the headpiece up under the ledge where it could stay—unless the water level drops significantly."

"Or?" he asks.

"Or, the natural hydraulic power will re-circulate the plastic."

"Forever?"

"Technically. If the souse hole is a keeper."

"A keeper?" Bertha asks.

"A keeper," I say.

"I like that idea!" she says.

"That's where Mr. Gilman is, then?" Adam asks.

Bertha sucks in her breath and folds the baggie to her chest.

"Probably not," I tell him. "You see ash isn't really porous. It's more like sand."

"I get it. So it'll travel and sink?" he asks.

"Yes. The ashes will keep going as part of the river system. The lighter parts stay within the flow. When the water goes down, the ash will settle. When the water flow goes up—"

"I like the idea of being washed over," Nemit says. "It's comforting."

"I don't know," Bertha says, backing away from us.

Nemit surrounds Bertha's shoulders with one lean, powerful arm and I am surprised when Bertha relaxes.

"I'll help if you'd like," Nemit says, gently.

Bertha rests her head on Nemit's shoulder and they glide over pebbles to the grey, muck-lined edge.

"My great-grandmother told me that committing her husband's body to the Ganges was an act of pure love."

"*Pure* love?" Bertha asks.

"*Pure love.*" Nemit replies. "You see he did not live the best life. He did not always treat my grandmother with respect. So, she washed him clean in the original river."

"But this is just the Bow," Bertha says.

"But here you are at its beginning where the water is uncontaminated."

Bertha unfurls her arms and the small bag rests in her palms like an offering. Nemit gently opens the top for her. Adam's thin arms circle my hips and his head rests against my ribcage. My breath is ragged, burns my chest and chokes in my throat. Bertha crouches and submerges the bag; Nemit's hand rests reassuring between her shoulder blades until she stands, empty bag dripping from her blue hands.

Chapter XI

I slip the yellow canoe between two narrow outcrops of sandy bank and watch it rock gently in the wash of the river.

"Why are we putting the boat in tonight?"

"Ritual," I say.

"Ritual?"

"I'm testing the water."

"You're superstitious."

"I always get the length of the canoe wet before I take it on a long trip."

"You're kidding."

"No. I'm quite serious. Joel and I always dipped the hull."

"Joel and you."

I straighten out of my squat next to the canoe and wrap the rope attached to the stern around my hand. Bertha's lips press together in a straight-line smirk; arms across her chest, she rocks back and forth on her feet. The sound of the frigid water lapping the sides of the canoe amplifies the quiet.

"Okay, let's heave it out," I say. I bend and hold on to the nearest strut. "What are you waiting for?"

"Joel."

I've given her an opening to bring up her favourite son-in-law.

"It's not bloody likely that he's coming, Bertha." My knees are straight and my knuckles look white against the pale wood.

"You're going to hurt your back!"

"Then help me!"

"Bend your knees!" Bertha commands. She lets her arms drop, steps forward, and glares at me.

"Grab the strut, would you? Bertha for God's sake—Jesus Christ Almighty!"

My mother likes to make me wait, likes to infuriate me. Gives her grounds to spar with me. She finally grabs hold and my straining hamstrings are thankful. Bertha is much stronger than her size suggests. She reminded me of just how strong when I tried to help her lift a four-gallon pail of paint one week before Ed's procession. My hand felt incidental next to hers.

"Finally. I hope I don't have to go through this at every portage," I say.
Bertha helps me ease the canoe from between the lips of earth and drag it onto the coarse grass.

"Imagine us carrying the canoe, four five-litre canoe bags, a Honda generator, and a tent across all the man-made breaks," I continue.

"What, not up to it dearie?"

"I'm more up to it than you and you know it," I say, laughing. "One more comment and the Honda stays behind."

"You like your creature comforts as much as I do. The Honda goes! Hey, why don't we leave the yellow banana boat right here? We know we can carry it for miles. Honest to God, the people on Bow Crescent must think we're touched."

"We're taking it back to the campsite, Bertha. Someone could steal it."

"They could steal it from outside the tent if they really wanted to."

"Here we go. Up, mother!"

"Up, mother," Bertha mimics. "Your neighbours must think we're nuts." We roll the canoe up on its edge. "No, correction. They must think I'm nuts and you are just mean." We each have one hand on the edge and one on a strut.

"Ready," I say. We crouch and heave together, lift the canoe over our heads, strut hands switching quickly to the outer edge.

"Gently," I grunt, arms adjusting. We rest the struts on our shoulders—use our hands to balance.

"For—ward, march!"

"I don't know why you don't let me do the front," Bertha says, intentionally switching feet so she's out of step with me.

"You'll be in the front when we paddle."

"Great—I'll get wet when we go through standing waves."

"Hah! You read some of the book I gave you! Don't worry, there's only one set of rapids tomorrow."

None of the other campers pay any attention to us. They gather around small fire pits or sit inside the glow of illuminated tents.

"Stay in step with me!" I sing.

"You're pulling," she says back.

"Then walk faster," I say. We cover the last fifty yards of black top and switch to the manicured gravel that designates our campsite.

"Have you ever wondered why—" Bertha says as I stop alongside the tent "—Parks Canada pays all those people to wear those God awful green—"

"Down."

"—And brown—uniforms?" The canoe shifts right, side parallel to the ground, "just to rake—"

"All the way, Bertha."

"—gravel in campsites? Shit!" She bangs the edge against her shin. "I have a permanent bruise there!" She lifts her pant leg. "Look! Is that not enough? And why is our tent set up on a cement pad?"

"The ground is sopping wet, that's the only reason we pitched the tent there. The pad is really for the picnic table."

"I don't see a table."

"They took them away. Too many bears."

"Bears?"

"They want people to use the cook shack out at the edge of the campground." Bertha stares at me, eyes big. "Remember the news a couple of years ago?" I say. "Two Swedes were mauled."

"Here?"

"Right here. Probably ate in their tent."

"Let's eat out," she says.

"We're camping."

"Let's eat at the Post Hotel." She knows I love to eat there. She mills around as I gather kindling for a fire.

"Careful, you're going to end up with wet feet," I say. "There's a hole off to the side of the cement pad. Let's get the generator going."

"We can't start *that* up in Lake Louise!" she whines.

"Then why'd we bring it?" I'm enjoying myself now. "We've got this tent that looks like a bloody house," I say.

"You wanted space—remember? You wanted two doors. The Honda is for down the river—when we get to those obnoxious campsites that border recreation areas—to keep the dirt bikers and the power boat people and the fly fishermen away." She hates quiet, which is exactly why she searched out and bought the small generator.

"They'll flock to us! The generator can light up a small village," I tease.

"Relax. It's only three hundred and fifty watts. Won't even run a hairdryer. You'll be glad for it in a few days when I plug in my little light, and Ed's mini stereo and play bagpipe classics."

"Not when we portage every dam and weir from here to Carseland three times!"

"We'll use it to scare people off! Shock bears!"

"Tell me that you don't have a tape player in your canoe bag." I know she does.

"You don't have a tape player in your canoe bag," she says. "But I do! Don't worry. I'll carry my own bags when we portage." There's no doubt in my mind that she's perfectly capable of carrying everything she's brought.

I drop a few logs next to the small fire pit. "Were you serious about dinner?" I ask.

"Post Hotel." She smiles, confident that she's won.

As we rummage in the tent for jackets and a flashlight I wonder why my mother and I don't just say what we mean. Earlier today Nemit got through to Bertha with a simple touch—and she made it look so easy. My mother is like a difficult teenager, confidence fluctuating, actions unsure. She jumps puddles on the way to the restaurant, one hand in her pocket. Why do I feel that our roles are switched? I note the gentle movements of Bertha's hand, the way she protects the contents of her pocket.

≈≈≈

"I went to a funeral yesterday, a lovely service for the wife of a friend. The whole event was staged—a designer celebration," I say as we take our seats in the Post restaurant.

"That's not how you saw Ed's funeral," Bertha replies.

"You're right. What you did today at the Bow headwaters was far more impressive."

My mother smiles at what I say. Touches my hand across the table.

"Menus," the waitress interrupts. "Can I offer you a drink to start?"

I order a bottle of Australian cabernet, assuming that Bertha will choose red meat.

"Joan arranged her whole funeral months in advance. Everything was colour coordinated. From the clothes she and her family wore to the flowers on her casket to the priest's purple cassock," I continue.

"Let me guess, cancer," she says.

"Yep. Brain tumour."

"There's a bloody epidemic, I tell you. Ed is one of the lucky ones. I want to go the way he did. Fast. No warning."

I agree with her, but I don't tell her. "Joan's daughter told me that her mother filled a book with instructions for the family."

"Funeral instructions?"

"*And* instructions on how to plant the garden, how the Halloween decorations should be placed on the driveway, where the large Thanksgiving turkey roaster is kept, lists of what goes where on the Christmas tree, lists of family birthdays and anniversaries—for both weddings and funerals."

"Sounds a bit anal, doesn't it?"

"Your wine, ladies. Have you had a chance to look over the menu?"

"No," we say together.

The waitress opens the bottle, pours a small amount and waits for my approval. She pours Bertha a glass and fills mine.

"A few more minutes then," she says, wiping condensation from the glass surrounding the candle in the centrepiece.

"A waste of time really," I say. "Her husband is selling everything and moving to a condo. He didn't want to tell her. Caught me and asked me to help him find one as I was leaving."

"What else did he say? Anything about his wife?"

"Not a thing. That was it. I didn't go to the wake."

"Very disappointing. Why not?"

"I felt strange there. Present absent."

"What do you mean?"

"Like the dead woman, right there in front of people but—"

"Ah—someone people look past. Lots of your old *friends* were there I suppose. Lots of them still together?"

"Yes. The whole thing was like a funeral for my past."

"*Your* past? How many people go to a funeral and think about themselves?"

"The widower was standing right behind me," I say.

"You make no sense, Marlo."

"The place was packed when I got there—two parking lots leaking cars onto the street, foyer full of people. I stood through the hour long mass—with Joel."

"Our Joel?" Bertha shrieks. "He's here and you didn't tell me!"

I should know better than to play keep-away with my mother. "He's here for a few weeks."

"Cancel the trip! Load up the canoe!" She thumps her fists on the table, wine spills.

"Everything all right, ladies?" the waitress asks, dabbing at the red stain.

"What's your name?" Bertha asks.

"Helena," she says, sponging the white tablecloth.

"Well Helena, I'm really hungry. What's the best thing on the menu?"

"Rack of Lamb with raspber—"

"We'll have two."

"Mum."

"My treat. Come on, you need protein to paddle."

"Thank you, ladies."

I wait until the waitress is a few feet away before I continue.

"He stood really close to me, laughing at the parts of the eulogy that were supposed to be funny. I felt—"

"I think we should call Nemit right now and have her pick us up."

"Bertha."

"How could you not tell me this? How could you let our boy come home and not tell me? — Where is he staying?"

"He's out at his parents'. We're not cancelling the trip."

"Longview. Longview. The Highwood right?"

"You're conniving, Bertha. We've talked about this before."

"Is he staying there for the whole time?"

"I don't know."

"I'm calling Joel up. We're having him over. Feel. How *do* you feel? Maybe he was happy to see you? Did he leave with you?"

I can't tell her anything—she's relentless. "It was an accidental meeting, Bertha. I had no idea he would be there."

"He *knew* you'd be there. Not just a coincidence—did you have lunch?"

"Our friend died. I attended her funeral. He attended her funeral. There is no *we.*"

"What was her name again? Nice service you said—the casket?"

"The most expensive."

"Was she buried?"

"Cremated."

"What a waste. Was it open?"

I love Bertha's fascination with macabre details. "No."

"Would it kill you to have lunch with him?"

"You're wasting your time, Bertha. It's like—"

135

"Blood from a stone. I know. Is he moving back?"

Our dinner arrives and I am thankful for the interruption. Disturbs Bertha's momentum. Lamb used to be a favourite with Ed and Bertha on a Sunday, Yorkshire pudding, thick brown gravy and mint sauce as well.

The waitress mops up the condensation pooling at the base of our wine glasses. "Everything all right ladies?" she says.

"Fine, just fine," Bertha says. "Let's cut the time to Calgary—we don't need to portage all those hazards. The ledges, the rapids, the wind on the reservoirs, and the currents caused by the dams, I'm not crazy about all that. Look, tomorrow we'll start early, paddle right into Banff in one day, get Nemit to pick us up at the canoe rental place—"

"And skip the portage around Bow Falls? The Banff Springs supplies porters when we stay the night. Aren't you forgetting the reason we are paddling?"

"No. How could you let Joel go?"

"Why can't you? No excuses, Bertha."

We concentrate on the meal cooling in front of us. Bertha pours more wine, drinks one glassful and then another before finishing her dinner.

My mother and I are complete opposites. She hangs on to people tooth and nail; I keep my distance. We journey together to let go: a travel oxymoron. People travel to get away, gain experience, collect paraphernalia, and meet new people. We travel to get home, to forget what we know, to cast off our belongings, and disconnect from people. Disconnect over and over. Why Bertha doesn't want to leave all of Ed in one place is beyond me. Four bags of ashes. Four stretches of river. Three more sprinklings to go.

"Can I take your plates, ladies? Bring you the dessert menu?"

"No," Bertha says, striking her wine glass with her fork, repeating a wedding tradition. "Is the roof leaking? Our tablecloth is damp."

"It's just the sweat from your water glass," I point out. "Drink up. We're paddling in the morning."

≈≈≈

Bertha's face is wet the day I marry Joel. Despite the location and the small crowd, she says she's happy. What every woman wants to know on her wedding day—that her mother is happy.

The main floor great-room of Assiniboine Lodge is a sea of heads when I walk carefully down the hand-cut staircase toward Ed's outstretched hand. The first time I married I resisted the mock up of the father *giving* his daughter away. The tradition implies ownership and, at nineteen and a half, I believed that no one had the power to own me. I walked down the aisle in the Longview Catholic church alone.

The first man I married was barely an adult. Domenic was a year younger than me, and working hard to pay off the property he'd purchased from his father when he was fourteen. I thought he was my match. By the time I turned twenty-one he was just a counterpart. I divorced him and left his lands intact. They were dry and worn out. I moved back to Calgary and my parents' home on the Bow.

Bertha and Ed are amazed that I ask them to accompany me when I marry Joel. I walk between them over wide creaking planks to where Joel stands with the JP. Bertha kisses me through her tears. Her fingers flutter on my empty belly. Ed's eyes and lips are parched.

"Proud of ye," he whispers before sitting next to Bertha. Through the whole ceremony I wonder why he says that.

The JP is married to a local sports announcer. She's vital and loud and looks strong as a horse in her Alberta Boot boots. Her Smithbuilt sports a feathered band, and the same feathers decorate and extend the length of her thick grey braid. Her long dress is loose at the waist and whiter than mine.

"Welcome!" she booms, extending her arms. Her voice forces its way through the chinks in the log walls and rushes out the open windows. For an instant I want to follow, but the stays in my dress keep me in place.

"Look about you—"

On that day I began a marriage that I wanted to last. Instead of hiding something old, something new, something borrowed or something blue under my dress and cloak—

"Take in the spirit of this sacred place."

I keep a secret.

"Internalize its power. Now look inside yourself."

Earlier my mother helps me cloak my vacant body—squeezes my hand.

"And join me in the commemoration of the unity matrimony brings."

Together we put the finishing touches on my costume. I step into crinolines that expand the folds of my extensive skirt. Bertha laces the back of my bodice and drapes me, shoulder to waist, in my husband's tartan.

"Stand now and circle this woman and this man with your intent, with your strength, and with your love," the JP continues.

Aunt Jane and my cousin Reed, Joel's mother and sister, Nemit and her partner Joy, and the group of Spanish seminarians who are staying in the lodge surround us. Joel gently raises my chin.

"Don't be afraid," he says, standing there tall and sure in his grandfather's Black Watch kilt.

He mistakes my behaviour for nerves. He thinks I'm overcome with emotion, which I am, but it's not wedding-induced. He removes the wool cloak from my shoulders and exposes my guilt-laden skin. He kisses the fingertips of my free hand, and past his shoulder I see Nemit's forehead touch Joy's.

The rest of the words intended to bring us legally together are of the usual kind—promises, assurances, undertakings, warnings and guarantees. Ed reads an overused passage from the Bible outlining why woman leaves her family and takes up with man.

We begin our vows. Only sheer luck disrupts the overpowering solemnity that hangs in the air. Ed and the soon-to-be Father Ibarra yell when the bad tempered cook roars outside the north windows. She frightens a black bear with a high-powered boat horn that threatens to rupture my eardrums—and I'm never really sure if Joel says, "I do."

Chapter XII

Bertha walks down to the river. She finds the cut in the bank that we used the night before and drops the first of the canoe bags and the generator on the grass. When she comes back, the tent and fly lie drying in the morning sun. I hand her a cup of milky tea and she holds it against her head.

"Something in it to take the edge off," I say.

"Ed's remedy?" she asks.

I nod and fold up the legs of the one burner stove, slip it into a bright blue padded sac.

"I only had three and a half glasses," she continues. "Can't drink anymore."

"You never were a big drinker, Bertha."

"How many glasses did you have?"

"About one and a half," I reply, sipping my tea from a speckled tin cup.

"Well at least I didn't go over the top about Joel."

I sit cross-legged on an insulated mattress and open the valve to expel the air inside. We both wear full wet suits with the tops turned down, fleece jackets and old running shoes.

"I'll make another trip," Bertha says, gathering up one more canoe bag, the small stove, and our life-jackets. She slips her arm through the two jackets, slings the bag over her shoulder, and dangles the stove from her other hand.

The jackets rub rhythmically across her shins as she walks away from me.

She rarely feels guilty about bringing up Joel but I know she's feeling sheepish this morning. I hoped that she'd let go of Joel, although he was the son she never had. Dug her garden, painted her fence, drove her out on stormy nights, attended mass with her every Sunday he was in town.

I roll the mattress and kneel on the surface to force the rest of the air out. Close the valve when I'm done and slip the mattress into another sac. Repeat the exercise again for Bertha's.

"How much longer?" she says when she's back. "I'm anxious to go."

"Let's carry the cooler next. We'll come back and fold up the tent, and that's about it, apart from our own bags."

Bertha takes the two rolled-up mattresses and I take the bag containing the items we plan to cast away. We lift the cooler together.

"Maybe I should take that bag, Marlo," she says.

"I'll be careful," I reply. "I know it's fragile. I have the makings of a box kite in there."

"A box kite?"

"A box kite. Remember the frame Ed made for me?" The cooler rocks between us.

"In Guides? You were twelve! And you call me a pack rat! What exactly are you planning to do with that?"

"Fly it of course!" I reply.

"Aren't there too many trees along the river?"

"I'm thinking of Johnston Canyon and the Ink Pots."

"A hike?" Bertha says.

"We'll want the exercise after sitting all day."

"I suppose," she says, as we set our cargo next to the bags she's already carried. "We haven't been there for years."

"The trail is busy to the first set of falls, but not too many people continue to the Ink Pots and beyond. Game?"

"Game!" she replies. "The fog is lifting. Let's get the tent, and the last two bags, then the canoe."

Bertha runs back to the flattened site and I try to follow at the same speed. My hips and knees complain, hate jarring against hard surfaces. Ran my body marathon thin five years ago and I still can't recover. My mother has better bones than I do.

≈≈≈

"Sixty-four," I say, cinching the last tie-down over our load.

"Not until next year, darling! Don't rush me," Bertha says.

"Kilometres," I say.

"Oh, isn't that a lot on water?"

"We'll be fine. About thirty-six to the campground today and twenty-eight tomorrow."

Her silhouette is missing the fanny pack and the auxiliary bits of Ed that I'm used to seeing bulge in her pocket. She looks free. Thin legs outlined in black rubber, yellow life-jacket still open in front, hair standing up in clumps all over her head.

"Ready?" she asks, teeth chattering.

"Ready steady," I reply. "Remember how to eddy out?"

"Yes." She distributes her weight evenly and stays low getting into the front of the canoe. She kneels, legs wide, fastens the clasps at the front of her life-jacket and pulls on gloves.

"Here's the extra paddle that we'll keep in the middle with the bags," I say.

"Where's the bailer?"

"Should be by your feet—at the front of the gear."

"Ah, got it. Okay Marlo, get in!"

"Hang on—the throw bag will sit there, just off to the side of the cooler," I toss it to her. "And here's the map case."

We're about fifty meters below the Louise rapids. We watch two kayaks negotiate their way through the boat-eaters. One paddler uses her whole body, swings her hips around a boulder and plunges through the standing waves at the end of the hazard. The other rolls, comes up and grounds himself on a gravel bar. The woman yips and pumps her paddle over her head, then removes her nose clip and yells at her partner to stick to the outside the rest of the way.

"I'm not sure that looks like fun!" Bertha says.

"Bloody well freezing!"

The woman waves to us and eddies out. She frees the spray skirt and steps onto the stony edge. Then she lifts the kayak over her head and begins the three hundred meter portage back to the parking lot further up the highway.

"Strong," Bertha says.

"Nah, those things weigh less than half what this canoe weighs. Remember what to do if we tip?"

"On my back, feet downstream," she says. "But I won't have to do that, will I Marlo? Submerging my body in water this cold will knock me out in less than three minutes."

"Eight or ten."

"Comforting," she says softly. "Shall we?"

I take in the forward line and throw it to Bertha. She uses her paddle to push the canoe away from the bank. With one foot in the canoe and one in the water I shove off. Bertha paddles for the middle, bow slightly downstream while I get seated in the stern.

"Stop paddling!"

Bertha holds her paddle ready while I sink mine and use it as a rudder. The current takes the front of the canoe.

"Paddle!" I say when we're almost parallel to the bank.

"Paddling," Bertha says, "paddling!"

We pull together.

≋≋≋

Headlines: *Marlo Isabel Gilman and Joel Adam Richards Cease to be Man and Wife*, or *Wife Disposes of Husband's Property*. Even: *Husband Terminates Contract With Wife*. The problem with the first is that it doesn't contain any leads. The problem with the second is that it misleads. The problem with the third—the third is true and untrue.

The charming Justice of the Peace, who goes to great lengths to marry me to Joel at Assiniboine Lodge doesn't register the marriage before Joel advises me he wants to make a quitclaim. Problem is, she is a certified Alberta official and Assiniboine Provincial Park is in British Columbia. Situated on the Great Divide.

After two years of property hunting and eighteen months of extensive renovations, after an additional two years of co-habitation and six and a half days of marriage, Joel asks me to remove all my belongings from the house—immediately.

"Go home to your mother," he says as if we live in another century and he can cast me off, legitimately, because I'm barren.

I am not barren. I did carry his child.

Separation, the ultimate form of abortion. Takes only one to initiate. Gestation time: less than one week.

"Does that break any Calgary Stampede records?" I ask Bertha at the time.

To make sure—absolutely sure—that he has no connection to me, Joel goes to St. Bernard's in Bowness, speaks to the nun in charge of annulments, writes a cheque for four hundred dollars, and insists that she rush the process.

"A rush?" she asks him. "Are you planning to marry again?"

He adds a four hundred dollar donation to the Sisters of The Perpetual Virgin "kick the habit" fund. Must have had her eye on a new pair of shoes. She searches the Alberta and British Columbia registries on the spot. Finds out that the marriage is not registered. A call to the JP is all it takes. We did not marry.

Recovery time: six weeks. No more blood spills between us. For the next nine months I refer to Joel as my un-husband. Then I move on.

≈≈≈

The river flows fast in July. Bertha and I reach the campsite below Johnston Canyon by two o'clock. The rapids I expect are only rolling waves at high water. Bertha does well. Doesn't get wet until we eddy out.

"Holy Mother of God!" she screams, as the frigid water engulfs her from the knee down. "Shit! The current—Marlo!" She fights to hold on to the front of the canoe, bent over, muscles straining for the seconds it takes me to swing the stern parallel to the bank. "I think we should eddy out the other way," she continues when I stand on the riverbed. "Parallel—together—like in the lessons."

I drop my paddle in the canoe and join her at the bow. We back up onto the bank and drag the canoe out of the water.

"Feet cold Bertha?"

"Understatement!" she says.

She sits down on the spot, takes her old runners off and pulls up the legs of her wet suit. Her skin looks blue. "Aren't you cold?" she asks.

"Yep," I say. "Let me grab our gear bags and we can put on dry shoes."

She rubs her hands vigorously up and down her shins, grabs one foot and pulls it up chest height, squeezes. Repeats on the other side. I loosen the tie-downs and pull out the bags we need.

"We can camp anywhere here," I say, looking across the small plateau we're standing on.

"I think we should pitch the tent close to the trees."

I pull the tent bag from the canoe. We decide on a grassy piece of ground with few rocks.

"There's a slight slope here and I hate sleeping with my head downhill."

"I don't think I'll care," Bertha says.

"Paddling takes more out of you than you think. Let's have a bite and rest for a while," I say.

When the tent is up Bertha disappears inside with the Thermarests. I peg out the fly and ferry the rest of our bags from the canoe. I divide the gear between the two vestibules, gently resting the small five-litre bag on Bertha's side.

"Okay," I say, unzipping the door on my side of the tent.

Bertha is sound asleep, gently wheezing the way Ed used to after a day in the shop, the Thermarests still in the long cylindrical bags under her head.

≈≈≈

The dowels that Ed cut for me all those years ago are still straight. The four longest pieces are thirty inches high, each notched and colour coded in four places: twice near each end, six inches apart. Sixteen smaller dowels each exactly fifteen inches long are marked with the same indelible colour code. *Grooves to tongues.*

I pull a small box of pin-like nails and a tiny tube of wood glue from the five-litre bag, the kind used in the balsa planes Ed and I flew over the river at the back of the old house. I fit four short pieces into four long sections, begin the frame, gently turn the skeleton over. The trick now is to repeat the exercise at the other end without the first coming apart. I'm unsuccessful.

I remember the recipe. *Build side one. Build side two. Join side one to side two, forming side three. Apply glue to each joint while building. Use small nails, one in each joint, to secure. Take care no' to split the dowel. Apply small amounts of glue to the remaining grooves in the frame. Carefully attach last four fifteen-inch dowels to complete kite. Gently tap in the last four nails.*

I make three bundles of dowel and hold them together with twist ties, squat next to the river and submerge the first bundle for five minutes, alternating hands to keep them submerged. Then I find a flat rock big enough to hold the other two in place. Moist wood is less likely to split when I nail the frame together.

I build side one. Two thirty-inch dowels and four fifteen-inch dowels. The glue holds. I lay the frame in the grass, retrieve another bundle and build side two the same way. I take the last bundle out of the water and glue four fifteen-inch dowels to side one, hold each in place for some time before moving on to the next. They stand perpendicular to the frame on the grass.

"Need a hand?" Bertha's sleepy voice.

"How long have you been watching me?"

"Long enough to see you add the last few posts."

She sits down, legs in a V, ready to hold the vertical sections while I attach side two.

"Why did you never build this kite with Ed?" she asks.

"I locked him in the garage—remember? Don't move!"

I leave her holding up the side I've just added, and retrieve my camera. When I come back the frame stands on its own, long edges on the ground. Side three up. I take a close up of Bertha lying on her stomach, looking through the frame at me. That black and white image is one of the last photographs I have. I give Joel a five by seven version the day I meet him to deliver Bertha's letter.

After I add the remaining dowels to close the frame, I use Ed's smallest hammer and sink sixteen tiny nails into the joints. Only one dowel threatens to split.

Bertha starts our one-burner stove and sets a pot of water to boil for pasta.

"How will I heat the sauce?" she asks.

"Pour the water out, add the sauce, and put the pot on the burner for a few minutes," I reply. "I'll look around for some wood for a fire and get back to the kite after we eat."

145

I make a pile of dead wood and split some of the smaller pieces for kindling. After we eat I bring out the fabric I'll use to cover the two end sections.

"Christ Almighty Himself!" Bertha shrieks. "Is that not the shift I dressed in a week ago?"

"What's left of it."

"But it's silk, Marlo."

"Excellent kite material! I've cut the bodice off about thigh level, no point in destroying the dress. I can hem the top and wear it! I only brought the skirt section."

Bertha chokes, expels the tea she's drinking through her nose and manages to repeat what I say. "The skirt—section."

She wipes her hand across her mouth and blows her nose toward the ground. I stare, fabric suspended between my hands. "I can't believe it!" she says, trying to gain control. "Where do you plan to cut the material?" She coughs, tries to clear liquid from her windpipe.

"On the canoe," I say.

"Jesus, Mary and Joseph."

After we eat we take the throw bag, bailer, paddles and lifejackets out of the canoe and turn it over. The hull settles to one side.

"Throw your wet suit over, inside out," I say. "Make sure it's completely dry for tomorrow."

I lay the dress section on the upturned canoe and cut the sides apart at the seams.

"My God," is all Bertha can say.

She holds the fabric taut as I cut eight-inch wide strips the length of the skirt.

"That does it, Bertha. I'll start the fire."

"Are you sewing tonight?"

"The light is still good. Sun won't set completely until nine-thirty or so. Want to help?"

"Will that start with a match?"

"One match," I say. The secret is in the fire starters, which I break up and push under the small pile of wood. Once the wood catches and I add a few bigger pieces, Bertha and I sit cross legged with the kite frame between us, sewing the silk around the box-like ends.

≈≈≈

Early in the morning we leave the tent to dry, hike to Johnston Valley carrying the kite and a small pack. We follow a path though the trees behind our tent, cross the highway, and walk toward the Canyon Lodge.

Bertha looks over at me.

"I know!" I say. "I also know that if I'd told you we were this close to a hotel, last night would have been quite different!"

"It was different."

We follow a paved path for about one kilometre to the lower canyon falls. The ten-meter drop seems just as incredible as it did when I was small. "Want to go into the cave?" I ask Bertha.

"I don't think so!" she says, shivering in the updraft the plunging water makes.

The kite warbles in my hand. We continue to the upper falls, climb a set of stairs that take us up and over the canyon lip. I'm careful, one hand on the rail, the other holding the kite. I keep an eye on Bertha, head down in front of me.

"The trail feels as if—it's been tamed," Bertha says, panting.

"By the time we—come back—we'll have to go through—crowds," I say. "So stick—to the inside wall—as much—as possible on the—lower trail."

We follow the white water and reach the upper falls fairly quickly. Bertha strides along the well-worn path that cuts through a stand of Douglas fir and lodgepole pine. I'm almost jogging, kite in both hands in front of me to keep up. She stands in the downdraft, hands on her hips like a Pan figure ready for take-off when I clear the trees.

"Twenty minutes!" she says. "Last time we were here you were ten. Ed and I had to run the whole way to keep up with *you*—Kite intact?"

"In—tact," I manage.

"Want me to carry it? Too heavy for you?"

I lead the way along another half kilometre of easy trail to a junction with a narrow access road. I feel the silk stretching off the frame, reaching out of Bertha's hands toward my back.

"How much farther, do you think?" Bertha asks.

"About two kilometres."

Bertha la-la's her way through a forest of white spruce and lodgepole pine. "Sing with me!" she bellows.

"I don't know the words!" I sing back off-key. "You're afraid of bears, aren't you?"

"I'm not afraaaid—of what I can't seeeee!" she wails at an operatic pitch that hurts my ears. The trail narrows as we reach the edge of the forest.

"Here!" she sings at the top of an incline. "You carry the kite."

"Is that the tune to 'God Save The Queen'?"

"Long live our noble queen!" she continues, marching.

We follow the rough path down into the meadows and stop once to drink before reaching the inkpots. Six natural Karst springs gurgle water up out of the ground at four degrees Celsius. We eat chocolate bars and apples while we examine the quartzite around the edges of each spring. The kite, which I set on the ground, tumbles off like a weed at the first hint of a breeze. Bertha catches up with it easily, gently grounds the box-frame.

"Time to fly." I take off my pack.

The end of a long veil, which I've rolled to the size of a volleyball, flaps from side to side. "Let's stand the kite on its end," I say to Bertha.

We kneel. I tie the end of the veil to the vertical dowel just below the top section of silk, twist it, and wrap it around the next upright. I do this three times before I let out a length and do the same thing at the bottom section of silk.

"You better tie it off," Bertha says.

I knot the veil to the base of the frame, then let out the rest to make the tail. The kite vibrates on the ground under Bertha's hands. One by one I extract five garters from the pack, cut them open and tie them at equal distances along the eager material.

"You are amazing, darling!" Bertha quips. The tail waves up and down, jerks at each tie.

"Just the string," I say.

"The wind is picking up!"

Calmly, I fix four equal lengths of nylon to the top and bottom corners, bring them together and tie them separately to an old metal key ring.

"What? No wedding band?" Bertha says.

"Got to save something for further down the river," I laugh.

I begin to knot the main string to the ring. The grass around us looks like it's running away. "It's ready."

"Not quite. Hold the kite!" Bertha pulls a baggie out of her fanny pack, pierces a hole in the plastic below the sealed top. She loosens the knot I begin to tie and cuts off a section of string, threads it through the hole. Knots it once, then ties the ends to the base of the frame next to the tail. She makes another small hole in the bottom corner. Grey matter trickles out.

"Hurry!" she says. She holds the kite down for the last time while I knot the main string.

"Ready."

Bertha stands with the top of the frame in one hand. The kite billows out behind her.

I run in the opposite direction, spooling the line out as I go. "Now!" I yell after letting out about thirty feet of nylon string.

She jumps and releases the kite. The string is immediately taut. I hold both ends of the spool loosely and let the wind decide how far the silk and veil will travel. Ed's ashes zigzag across the horizon in front of Castle Mountain. Then they are gone. Bertha turns to me, hand over her mouth just as the end of the string takes flight.

Chapter XIII

I have trouble with endings. I have trouble staying composed on the hike back. I'm in front of Bertha most of the time, listening to her account of the flight over the meadow. I like endings to remain whole and undistorted—like fairy tales. When Bertha prompts me for stories about how my marriages end, I tell her, "There's nothing to say." But there is something to say about beginnings. Beginnings interest me more than endings. Whenever Bertha asks me about Domenic or Lynn, Jack, Raj or Thomas, I stick to the beginnings.

"What about the house in Inglewood?" she says, after I've listened to the post-flight report.

The home that Joel and I renovate during our years together is still mine. He and I manage a beginning while we live there. I cannot bring myself to sell that home. It's the only location, the only piece of property *I* engage with.

"Still not sold," I reply. "Watch out for the crowds down there," I say as we descend the stairs and retrace our steps on the paved path to the trailhead. It's impossible to hold a conversation and I'm thankful.

I convince Joel to buy the house in Inglewood before living in *that* end of town appeals to many Calgarians. The Deane House is newly restored and Fort Calgary is still without its interpretive centre when we move onto New Street.
The old two-storey house is small and run-down, and the first building our friends see when they come to visit after entering the neighbourhood from downtown is strung with fishing poles, hip waders and inflated rubber dinghies. They feel sorry for us and think we've fallen on hard times—until they shop in Barotto's or spend the afternoon in the long back yard watching the river. The house becomes a neighbourhood curiosity when we begin to renovate, add scaffolding to the outside; it's the place people stop when they overshoot the old zoo turn-off.

"God, I'll be glad when we leave this trail!" Bertha hollers over the small crowd of people between us. "I never thought I'd say this," she yells, "but let's get in the damn canoe!"

≈≈≈

Bertha screams. Blood curling sounds penetrate the forest around us and attract the attention of a bus full of tourists stopped to photograph the Bow Valley at Red Earth Creek. Glacial water pours in over the front of the canoe.

"Paddle!" I yell. "Bertha, paddle or we'll go right in!"

She strokes despite the fact that she kneels in a pool of greenish water that's two degrees above zero.

"Hard! Pull to the inside!"

I move from my seat and kneel as low as possible inside the yellow body of the canoe. She pulls hard. If she doesn't we'll go wide and drop over a small ledge.

"Mar—lo! Maar—loo!" she screams.

More water spills over the bow. We float-turn as if the waves are smooth, as if the canoe is weightless. Then the hull, suddenly heavy, bangs against the surface.

I fight to keep the stern from coming around, feel afraid. Bertha leans as far as she dares. My collarbones rub against my life-jacket and my shoulders shake uncontrollably. "Eddy right!" I call.

We lunge-paddle as if driving a dragon boat in a still water race, beach the canoe on the gravel outcrop at the end of the rapids. Our body weight flies forward. Speed we gain through the rapids suddenly meets the inertia of dry land. The crowd in the parking lot is out of sight, but a few brave souls run along the portage route to see if we make it. A man in uniform and two others sporting cameras return my wave. I look downstream until the echo of their feet on the hollow ground stops.

"Get out, Bertha," I say. She's still kneeling in the bow.

I get out and help her. Her lips are blue and her hands shake. The fact that she's quiet disturbs me. I pull off my lifejacket and she sits on it. Her feet and lower legs have no colour. I rub one, then the other until she tells me I'm hurting her. I take her pulse. Normal.

"F—fuck," she says before standing up and walking around. She shakes her legs and arms out like a runner preparing for a race.

I use the bailer to empty as much water from the canoe as possible.

"Is the gear wet?"

"There's a bit of water left in the middle but nothing inside the bags is wet." I check the hard plastic case containing my camera. "Everything is just fine," I say.

"Wh—what about Ed?" She stammers.

I unfurl the top of the small canoe bag. "Dry as a bone!" Two baggies stare up at me.

≈≈≈

Forty minutes earlier we got into the water below the Johnston Canyon campground. Twenty minutes after that we stopped to assess the rapids. We decided not to portage.

"They're class three at low water, class two now," I said. "I know we can make it, Bertha. Joel and I have paddled this section three or four times."

"All right," she agreed. "If Joel thinks it's safe, it must be safe. I don't relish the thought of emptying the canoe when we just packed it a little while ago."

I always forget that my mother is not my age. I forget that there are some things that affect her body more than mine. She takes all day to warm up despite the fact that the temperature above the surface of the water is twenty-five degrees Celsius. She shivers in spite of the effort required to cross the deep stand-still water of Vermillion Lakes, after we go under the bridge and continue on the south side of the Trans Canada Highway. Bertha doesn't warm up until she's soaking in a hot tub in the basement of the Banff Springs Hotel.

≈≈≈

The porters wait for us at the historic boathouse. We see the limousine pull up while we paddle the deceiving current between Vermillion Lakes and Bow Falls; the slow deep water says nothing of the danger ahead.

We watch two men in burgundy vests light cigarettes and lean against the black hood. Locals and tourists crowd the car, peer at the dark glass, look for a famous face.

"What's going on?" Bertha asks, pointing her paddle.

"That's our car."

"How do you know?"

"I see the poles of the canoe trailer sticking up behind the trunk."

Luke and Michel welcome us to Banff, take our arms and escort us to the car. The leather seats are draped with rough wool blankets edged in red, yellow and green, thick covers purely for show on a day like today, but Bertha wraps herself in one, waves like the Queen Mother in a carriage, poses like Garbo, and lets a woman on Bear Street photograph her profile.

"You are like a little doll!" Michel tells her, as he guides her rubber-clad body into the hotel lobby.

≈≈≈

Do you ever feel comfortable when you undress in front of your mother? I always want to scream, *don't look at me*. Instead, I slip into the hot water and feel my face turn deep red.

"That was an uneventful day," Bertha says over the low rumble of the water jets.

"Uneventful?"

"Yeah. Almost boring. Except for the part where you tried to kill me."

I can't take my eyes off her small cherry-red nipples as they dance in the swirling water. Her breasts don't fold over her rib cage like mine do. We sit in the deep pool in the ladies' spa. Two robes and two bottles of French water are within easy reach on the tiled floor.

Bertha sinks under the water. When she comes up she makes eye contact with me. "You've gained a few pounds," she says. "That's good."

"Everything looks bigger under water."

"Unless the water is cold," she says. "Did you see the look on the faces of the people paddling in front of the Banff Boathouse today?" She sips the expensive water and adds, "Someone should bottle the Bow."

"A limousine pulling a canoe trailer is pretty unusual!"

"It felt so good to sink back in that leather seat, even if the ride only took eight minutes."

"You timed it?"

"Of course," she replies. "Add twelve minutes to check in, pretty unusual if you ask me, I think they wanted us out of the lobby. Add twenty-three for the bags to come up to our room, that's forty-three. Forty-three is the number of years Ed and I were married."

She closes her eyes and dips under the water again. I take the opportunity to get out and wrap myself in a robe. Forty minutes from the start of our day trip to the time Bertha's legs submerge in freezing water.

≈≈≈

The telephone rings as we open the door to our room.

"Where have you been?" Nemit's voice shrills.

"Oh, we were just soaking," Bertha says, into the mouthpiece. "I got you the price list and the rates for a day in the spa are very reasonable."

I take the phone from her.

"Didn't you get enough water today?" Nemit says.

"Don't tell me you're worried. You know how many times I've been on the Bow."

"Not with your mother! Is she all right?"

"She's fine," I say. "She got a little wet at the beginning of the day, but—"

"Marlo!"

"She's fine."

"We're meeting you for brunch tomorrow, right?"

"Exactly as planned."

"We're bringing you a gift," she says.

"A what?"

"Something very practical that you can take with you for the next section. Haven't changed your mind about paddling across all those man-made lakes?"

"Nope."

"She's too old."

"Nonsense," I say. "She's in better shape than I am."

"Thanks darling!" Bertha says, from the telephone in the bathroom.

≈≈≈

I'm pleased and surprised. The gift is a collapsible canoe trailer. I pick it up.

"Only nine kilos," Adam says proudly. "I found it in the canoe shop on Bowness Road."

"It's wonderful!" I say.

"Good for up to three hundred and fifty pounds," he adds.

We stand in front of the famous hotel, canoe bags in a pile, waiting for Nemit's car. Bertha and I are dressed in our wet suits. She holds the five-litre canoe bag in her left hand. Nemit holds her right hand. Two porters struggle up the stony drive with the canoe. They carry it awkwardly, right side up.

Adam runs toward them, pulling the mini trailer at the end of the long tie-down straps. He motions to the two porters. They set the canoe on the padding and watch, arms folded over their chests, as Adam steers the contraption to where we wait.

"Easy!" he calls.

"You won't have to strain," Nemit says to Bertha.

"Pneumatic tires," Adam says.

"You are very thoughtful, dear," Bertha says to Nemit, repeating a phrase my Granda often used.

Chapter XIV

My grandfather read romance novels when he was eighty-eight. Pored over them with an intensity I'd never seen before. He took the old teak and canvas deck chairs down to the riverbank, set them up side by side and didn't come in until the book was done. Read one a day every day of the week except Sunday, the empty chair always next to him. Loved old Canadian stories involving exploration, hard women and vindicated men.

Michael Gillman loved the river. Said it reminded him of the ocean that rimmed the dried-up property he quit in the north of Scotland near John O'Groats. He passed his love of moving water on to Ed. I caught Ed reading one of Granda's novels once. *Signed, Sealed and Delivered* it was called. Had a picture of a woman in a buckskin jacket and gloves on the cover. A man kneeling in a canoe filled the background. Bertha says she recently found that same book in the middle of a stack of *Car and Driver* on her bedroom floor.

Have you ever wondered at the depth of connection people have to each other? Sometimes I look at Bertha and I think she's free of Ed and then I find her smelling his clothes or wearing his huge watch on her tiny wrist. Two days before we began this canoe trip she built a wall of magazines between the end of their bed and the bedroom door. Says she found an article on Feng Shui, which advises that the knife-edge of the door should not compromise the bed.

"There's a difference," I say, "between a screen and a wall."

I think about Granda and Ed as the west wind pushes us across Lac Des Arcs.

"Ugly, isn't it," Bertha motions to the scarred mountain with her paddle. The rock looks like a magnified well bore. I think her heart is cored the same way.

"Ugly is an understatement." Smoke billows from the cement plant stacks. I feel like a character in a B-movie.

"I wonder when mining limestone became important?" Bertha asks.

"When the coal ran out. Before that people used to drive up from Calgary and load up their wagons. Later, they filled their car trunks with boulders, trundled back, used the stone to build basements."

"Build basements?"

"Build basements. The man who manufactured the first Greyhound bus in Calgary hired the vehicle out to an Italian stonemason for the test run. The bus carried tons of limestone."

"Wonder how much that cost?"

"Nothing for the stone, but the mason had to pay thirty-five cents for each hour that it took his men to load the stone."

"And you know this because?" Bertha asks.

"I know this because Thomas' grandfather built the bus. He owned the Greyhound shop. Bought it with the other shop men during the Depression."

"True story?"

"True story. The shop was on the river lot west of the Centre Street Bridge." The wind changes, comes over the port side. We have to lean hard into the inconsistent gusts.

"Who—owns the lot now?" Bertha gasps.

"The Calgary—Chinese Sen—iors—Society. Thomas' family paid off their homestead with the money they made when they sold it—careful!" When the wind dies the canoe rocks dangerously.

I press against the mud three feet below the surface with the flat of my paddle. "Stop!" I yell, trying to centre my weight. "Paddle!"

"They still have the homestead, right?"

"Thomas owns it! His Grandfather mortgaged the house so they had collateral for the Greyhound shop."

"Little Bow right—that your territory?"

"No!" We're closing in on the end of the lake. The wind is powerful and we fight to stay off the rocky shore until we reach the portage. "Draw!" I call to Bertha, but my voice is lost before it reaches her.

She looks back for a moment, then completes the move. Her short hair dances on top of her head. "So—thought—ful," she says, as we pull the canoe onto the bank.

"Thoughtful?" I say, my breath ragged.

"Nemit," she says, fingering the canoe cart.

I throw my lifejacket next to the gear, fold the cart frame out and snap the locking mechanisms in place.

"Can we lift the canoe?" I ask, standing back, hands on my hips.

"Let me get the low end," Bertha moves down the slope. "If we can't manage, we'll take a few things out."

I reach in and set the generator aside.

"The heaviest thing is the cooler," Bertha says. "Let's heave that out, then we'll be set."

"Without even trying?" I ask.

"Without even trying," she replies. "No point in you throwing your back out this early in the day!"

We block the wheels with rocks, front and back, then we heft the canoe onto the trailer after Bertha lifts the cooler out.

"Forward a bit!" Bertha cries. "Come back here and help me push. Don't try to pull!"

We balance the canoe and I fasten the tie-downs. Bertha puts the cooler and the generator back. We start along the bumpy trail.

"Slowly," I caution. Ever tried to negotiate a three-foot wide trail with a sixteen-foot canoe on a trailer? Bertha gently touches the five-litre bag, then pushes from the back. I guide the front away from overhanging branches. The wind blows, blusters, and sighs around us.

≈≈≈

My father's body sighs with relief an hour after he dies. The sound startles me.

"Natural occurrence," the Paramedic says.

159

Neighbors carry Ed from the driveway in front of my parents' home after his collapse. He lies on his back, eyes not quite closed when I arrive. Paramedics have to yell and pull at Bertha before she stops CPR. They take her to the kitchen. I sit with Ed, insist the medical team wait another hour and forty minutes before they move him.

I notice the wedding ring he never wears standing dust-free on the bedside table. Bertha cleans it weekly as if it's one of her precious china ornaments. Ed insists it's dangerous to wear a ring in his line of work. I look at the third finger of my left hand, collapsed by the weight of four rings. I kneel next to the bed and spread my hand over Ed's. It's the only time I label him, "Father." I stand heavily when the priest's black frock invades my peripheral vision. Listen to Bertha sob through "The Prayer for the Dead."

≈≈≈

"Jesus, Mary and Joseph!" Bertha screeches at the sight of two dozen crows on a tree beside our next launch. "What do you think that means?"

"Probably a dead animal around somewhere. Hunters."

"I thought the Bow was just popular with fly-fishing types."

"Fishing isn't as popular on the upper Bow. The water temperature and the silt during run-off make fish difficult to find."

"What kind of fish? Salmon?" Bertha looks nervously at the black flock.

"Whitefish and varieties of trout. We may see people fishing closer to the Seebe Dam."

"Ed came ice-fishing with Joel once, didn't he?" She stumbles over the uneven trail, her neck bent at a strange angle so that she can keep the birds in sight.

"They went to Hector Lake."

"Stayed at Nakoda Lodge?"

"The Stony Nation keeps the lake stocked. You can fish for a fee."

"Can we go to the lodge for something to eat?"

"Why are you always thinking about your stomach, Bertha?"

We stop at the top of a steep bank, block the cart wheels, and look for the best way to get the canoe down. Bleak images of cold rock and frigid water inhabit my mind today. Even when the Seebe-Exshaw area is hot there's a coldness about the place. Maybe it's caused by great gusts of cold resident in the gaping holes in the mountains—updrafts from dead-end mine shafts. Perhaps the disruption of the natural flow of the river gives the region a stilted feel. I've hunkered at the tops of Lady MacDonald, Ling Ha, Heart Mountain and Grotto Mountain. The vista is fantastic but the wind lets you know that you're not welcome. The only place that warms me is Grotto Canyon. The rock floor and walls send heat through the body.

I turn to see a man with jet hair standing at the end of the canoe. Makes no sound but startles me just the same.

"Never saw a canoe with wheels," he says.

Bertha grabs my arm. A rifle rests in the crook of his left arm.

"Don't worry," he adds, "it's not loaded." The breast pockets of his dark blue jean jacket bulge with ammunition. "What's it made of?"

"Aluminum," I say.

"That canoe," he replies, barrel to yellow.

"Kevlar."

"It's as thin as a skin." He circles the canoe, runs his free hand along the sides. "Stands up to rocks, does it?" He sets the gun on the ground, caresses the seam at the front with both hands. "How much's it worth?"

"Twen—" Bertha starts before I cut her off.

"Hunting deer?" I ask.

"Elk."

I gauge the face, take in the shadow of stubble, note the well-known brand of outdoor shoes and the micro fiber pants he wears.

"Zip off to shorts," he says. "Never used that option yet. Too many insects."

"Interested in a vest?"

"A vest?" Bertha asks.

"A vest," I repeat. "Kevlar. Just like the canoe, only thicker. Can stop a bullet."

"Let me see, then."

I pull the five-litre bag from our bundle of gear and retrieve Lynn's camouflage vest.

"Adam likes to wear that!" Bertha says. She takes the bag from me and hugs it to her chest.

I hold the vest like a coat, inviting. The man turns, puts his hands through the armholes. The vest doesn't quite reach his waist, fastens easily over the lean chest. He sinks three fingers in the cylindrical tubes on the front.

"How much, then?" he asks, as if we're standing in the middle of a car lot.

"Nothing," I say.

"Oh, no!" he says. "Gotta be somethin'." He whistles. A girl, about Adam's age, emerges from the brush carrying a fishing rod and a small cooler. The man motions to her. She leaves the rod against a tree and takes the lid off the cooler. Two good-sized brown trout stare up out of crushed ice.

"That do?" he asks.

"Very nicely," I say.

Without another word the girl picks up the fishing rod, the man retrieves his gun, and the two disappear behind the green canopy.

"Mother of God!" Bertha says. "Are those fish safe to eat? They sure are ugly."

"They're safe to eat."

"But isn't the water polluted here?"

"It's better here than downstream from Calgary. There, fishermen catch and release most of the time."

We decide to unload some gear before we ease the canoe, which is still on the trailer, down the steep slope to the river. The terrain is as good as it can be. Hasn't rained in some time. We decide that we'll both stay at the up-hill end.

"Remember Marlo, use your legs, not your back."

"Thanks, B!"

She lets go and the only way I can keep the canoe from hurtling down the eight or nine feet in front of us is to sit down, arms pulling out of their sockets.

"Don't call me that! Do you know how many times Ed—?"

"I didn't mean it like that! Help me or I'll have to let go!"

"Christ Almighty!"

She hangs on to me as the crows take flight.

≈≈≈

It's a short seven kilometres to Seebe and the Horseshoe Dam where we'll leave the river and wait for Nemit. She convinces me at brunch there's no way I can expect Bertha to manage all the hazards, natural or man-made, between Seebe and Calgary. Too risky to deal with the sudden increase in flow caused by the utility company, to portage the dams, negotiate rapids and ledges, or paddle the gales on the Ghost Reservoir. We'll stop the car and look at the Horseshoe Falls with Nemit and Adam.

"What about some lunch?" Bertha asks as we carry the gear down the slope to where the canoe is grounded.

"It's not far to Seebe," I say. "Let's eat when we get there."

She pouts for the next six minutes, lifts our cooler lid after mustering it down the slope, and takes out a few slices of headcheese. She makes long rolls with the meat and munches on it slowly while I ferry the remaining gear.

"Let's get going," I say, when I secure the last tie down.

"Paddling won't be that difficult."

"I know, the next section of river cascades near the highway, but the wind will take a lot out of us."

Today is Thursday and traffic is minimal. A bright red truck slows and stops at a picnic rest stop. The man who exchanged the fish for Lynn's vest gets out. He smokes and watches us until the river bends away and disappears between dark green forests.

"So," Bertha says after a while. "Will I ever know why you kept that hunting vest? Or why Lynn left in the middle of the night?"

"I don't think I should tell you, Bertha."

"Why not?"

I don't answer her right away. I think about why not, about my attachments to endings and I decide it's time to let the story go. The vest is gone. The ring he gave me is mangled. The silk damask I wore the day we married is probably lining an animal den or bird nest by now.

"Okay," I say, looking downstream at the back of her head. "I held a gun to his head." The canoe rocks violently and Bertha drops her paddle in the river. "Forty days after the marriage he came into the bedroom wearing nothing but that Kevlar vest." Bertha picks up the paddle. "I thought he was playing hunter. We wrestled. I crouched on all fours, then I felt a cold barrel between my shoulder blades. I didn't see the revolver. He'd tucked it in the pouch on the back of the vest. As soon as it touched my skin he lost his erection."

"Jesus, Mary, and all the saints in heaven preserve us," she whispers. "If Ed knew."

"Later, when he was asleep, I stashed the vest in the basement freezer and retrieved Granda's old shotgun."

"Mother of God! It's an antique! You don't know anything about guns!"

"I know that particular model does a lot of damage." I paddle rhythmically. "I held it to his head and I waited for him to wake up. He thought it was another game. I told him to get dressed. He did, smiling. I motioned to the bedroom door. He walked through. I followed and nudged him. He skipped down the stairs. I pointed to the open patio door with the barrel. He went out and turned a pirouette on the lawn. I motioned to the garage. He went through the side door. The big door was open and his truck was running on the driveway. He slid onto the passenger seat, moved it back as far as it would go. I watched him open his fly before I told him to leave."

"He didn't ask any questions?"

"He said, *Sorry?*"

"What about his guns?" Her hands grip her paddle, which is flat across the gunwale as she twists in her seat to stare at me.

"Stroke," I say. She manages two or three before she turns around again. The skin on her neck is taut. Looks like it will tear. "I closed up and went inside. Called the local constable to confiscate the guns. Any person who lives in a place where there are firearms can have them removed."

"Just like that?"

"Every home containing a registered firearm is supposed to get a call from the police department. When the owner moves from place to place, *if* they register a change of address, the new place gets a call. They phoned when Lynn moved in. They asked if I felt threatened. If I'd said yes, they told me, they'd come and confiscate the firearms. That night I called the district office."

"Jesus Christ, Marlo! The non-emergency number?"

"Three officers came and emptied the gun case."

"No questions? You had to tell them the *details?* How could you not tell us?"

"One officer stayed in a car about half a block down the street. The other two waited in front of his office building. Lynn showed up at home, feet still bare. He was escorted away with all of his belongings."

"Nemit came to stay."

"Yes."

"We thought she—converted you! We asked Sister Margaret and Father Joe to visit you."

"They did. There's a bend coming up."

She starts to paddle again, sporadically. "Six months later Thomas invited you to the farm. Why couldn't you tell me? I'm your mother."

"I just did."

Bertha paddles the last two kilometres muttering. *Ed...Why...Nemit...Sons-of-bitches.*

I smile.

≈≈≈

We reach the west side of the Horseshoe Dam an hour or so before Nemit. We walk up to the parking area anyway. It's empty. We decide to stay by the river and cook the fish. I collect dead wood and before I start the fire Bertha hugs me. Holds me. Feels as if she's making up for something.

"You are the strongest and also—the most stupid woman I know."

"Come by it honestly," I say to her eyes.

I build a small pyre of twigs, reach inside the five-litre bag, which now looks deflated without the kite makings, the veil, the garters, the vest, and two bags of Ed. I take out a pearl-finished bridal missal.

"Jane gave that to you when you married Thomas!" Bertha says, horrified.

"No. When I married Raj," I say. "She objected to his religion. Wanted to make a point."

Bertha stomps around, bangs a small pot onto the stove.

"Won't you need water?" I ask.

She takes out the large clear plastic jug full of Calgary water.

"You could use river water since you're going to boil it."

"No point in taking any chances," she scowls at me.

I know she admires the gold edges and the silk ribbon of the traditional prayer book, but I enjoy tearing the page with spaces for the bride and groom's names away from the threaded binding.

She spills water over her dry runners.

I crumple the page and tear out five others before I strike the match. I feed the little blaze with crumpled pages until I can add bigger, dryer pieces of wood.

"That's sacrilegious," she says.

"Rice nearly ready?" I ask.

She calms down watching me prepare the fish. I decide to cook the smaller one. It's about three pounds.

I pull out the folding knife that Joel gave me as a gift. I can't for the life of me figure out the contradictions that form Bertha's outlook. When Ed dies she quits the Church. Doesn't go to mass for—three weeks. Then she goes back. Goes every day for the next four months. Self-imposed penance.

I expose the blade. Bertha tries to get me to go too. Says I have no excuse since I don't work in the early mornings. I only give in on Sundays.

I insert the tip of the blade in the throat. "Head on or off?" I ask her.

"On," she says.

She squats next to me. Runs a fork around the inside of the rice pot then sets it on the ground. Winces at the sound of the knife tearing the delicate flesh, her pelvis bouncing as she adjusts her stance.

"Bones now or later?"

"Later," she says.

I spread a doubled length of foil on the ground. Fold in the edges to make a tray. "Get the butter," I say as I submerge the fish in the river, empty the guts and the contents of the bowels in the flow. Better than dust to dust.

She smears butter on the foil while I pat the inside of the trout dry with some paper napkins that I then add to the fire.

I lay the fish on the aluminum.

Bertha sprinkles dill, lemon pepper and salt on the flesh. Fills the cavity with the rice and two knobs of butter. Folds the foil carefully around the gashed belly. Seals the ends. She hands the packet to me.

I place it cautiously on the grill, which I've just set over the gray-flaking wood. I balance the packet quickly so I don't scorch my hands, keep the heat steady by adding small amounts of wood to the hottest sections of the fire. Bertha watches me for a while then walks along the riverbank as far as she can.

I put the condiments and the roll of foil away. Putter about, move gear that doesn't need to be moved. I look upstream. She's praying, head bowed, hands clasped upside down at thigh height.

I split the plastic missal cover with the axe. Bertha looks up at the cracking noise. I stride toward the canoe, retrieve a garbage bag. Can't imagine spoiling the fish.

"Incinerate the whole thing?" she asks when she comes back.

"I think the fish will be ready pretty soon. Not even sticking to the foil."

I turn the packet over using two long branches.

Bertha takes a baggie from the inside pocket of her jacket. I watch as she trickles the contents into the fire. The grate moves. Blue smoke swirls. I stretch out my arms and pull the smell to my chest. Rest my hands for a moment. Dust settles against Bertha's rubber-clad legs. The smoke subsides.

"Is it Friday today?" Bertha asks.

"Thursday," I say.

"Then I won't worry about having fish tomorrow."

Contradictions. I jostle the packet onto a plate and gingerly open it, peer inside.

"The bones should just peel away now," Bertha says, watching.

"They're here, Mom!" Adam screams, as he runs full tilt down the slope. He throws his arms around my neck, kisses me. "The canoe cart works?"

"The canoe cart works," I say, play-punching his shoulder.

Bertha walks towards Nemit and embraces her.

"I know, I know," I hear Nemit say, as they stand next to the fire.

"I can't wait to call Joel!" Bertha says, over her plate of food five minutes later.

Chapter XV

I'm not surprised to see Joel's tall frame in Bertha's front window. I've come to drive her to mass. I knock and open the door on their laughter.

"Hi Marlo. I won't join you for mass," he continues, turning to Bertha, "but I'll see you again before I fly out."

He stands and hugs her. Do you ever wonder why your friends and lovers embrace your mother? Maybe they are compensating. Maybe there's a connection, or a cross-generational attraction. Maybe Bertha feels as if she's reaching me even when I won't let her.

"Drove by the old house," he says. "Let me take it off your hands."

"You're moving back?" I ask.

"In a month," he says. "Think about it!" Joel kisses Bertha on the cheek and leaves.

"Nice breakfast?" I press bacon crumbs onto my fingertips.

"Very nice, dear. You should have come."

"You didn't invite me."

I ask her to hurry up. Before we drive off, she leans a worn leather briefcase against the back of the car seat. For the next hour I go through the perfunctory motions of standing and sitting and kneeling. Bertha tries to engage me in whisper talk but I resist.

I can't picture anyone in the Inglewood house, resist buyers for nine years. Now I picture Joel—filling the planters with miniature arctic willow, stretching for a map, climbing the metal stairs. Hair much shorter, body over-worked to retain its youthful hardness.

Bertha pokes her finger into the softness covering my belly.

"Why so somber?" she asks. "Mass is over, dear, wait for me in the car. I need a moment or two with Father Joe."

She strides towards the business office. I wait for the crowd to clear before engulfing myself in outdoor light.

When I drop her off she says, "I'll be over at seven-thirty tomorrow, as planned." Her hair radiates a purple glow where the sun penetrates its thickness.

"Okay."

"Wait! I'll give you the canoe bag to fill," she jogs inside, briefcase flapping. The MG sputters and coughs.

I'm revving the motor when she comes back.

"Hang on!" She thinks I'm in a hurry. The bag is open. Contains one ingredient: Ed. "See you in the morning," she says, repeating a line Joel used when we first met.

≈≈≈

"Let me take it off your hands," Joel says. Just like that. No thought, no careful consideration of what I might feel. What am I feeling? He's thought about where he wants to live! He is careful, he is considerate—was. Did he cover the details as I did? Did he check the property for liens? One previous marriage. Did he inspect the structure? Carefully fed body. The heating system? Good circulation. The electrical box and wiring? Sound mind. The neighborhood? One of the oldest in Calgary. The neighbors and friends? Many. Did he consider the family? One father, one mother.

I decide that I mirror my mother. My corrupt imagination stands in front of me like one of her contradictions. I'm in the basement of my home. I stare at the dress I design to include the most critical elements of bridal style. The dress I wear the day I don't marry Joel. The only dress I panic about, fret and fuss over. I consider neckline options: off-the shoulder, jewel, Queen Anne, illusion, bateau, wedding band, scoop, V, and sweetheart. Sleeve styles: short, sleeveless, long, fitted, Juliet, and leg-o-mutton. The train: sweep, chapel or cathedral. The fabric: silk chiffon, crepe, taffeta, damask and peau de soi; I mull over duchess satin and tulle. The headpiece. I think headband, garland, tiara, full or half circle, comb, crown, or hat. The veil. I contemplate Madonna and birdcage, flyaway, elbow, fingertip, and chapel length, blusher, and mantilla. I take care with the shoes, the stockings, and the lingerie. I wear a merry widow, I borrow Bertha's earrings, and the ribbon trailing from my bouquet is blue.

The gift for the groom dangles from the neck of the dress form: one sixteen-inch chain and small oval Saint Christopher in ten-carat gold intended to protect the traveller. I put it on.

I examine the hem and skirt for stains. The peau de soi is un-marked in spite of the trek I make from Inglewood to Bowness. I am wearing the dress, admiring my reflection, when Joel asks me to leave. The off-the-shoulder bodice is no longer discolored by the sweat that runs between my breasts and trickles from my underarms.

Bertha saves the gown. Submerges the layers in her bathtub. Watches the fabric bubble and float. Wears gloves to treat the stains. Carries it dripping and un-wrung to the basement of the old house.

I remember the dress hanging from the floor joists by long threads carefully drawn through the shoulders, the waist, and the back of the hem. Bodice packed with white kitchen catchers to help keep its shape. Skirt wide as a church bell. The dress dancing in the artificial wind whipped up by the caged blades of two large electric fans.

I imagine the platinum wedding band resting on my ring finger. I stare, the coincidence of lines that construct the altar cross pattern come to life on my skin. The ring only becomes the bride's property when she exchanges her body for a marriage certificate. I give up my body for a few months, but I don't own the metal band Joel designs.

≈≈≈

I drop a set of twelve stainless steel forks in the five-liter canoe bag. The bundle looks meaningless next to the remaining baggie that Bertha seemed glad to give me yesterday. The bag is vacant. I decide to use a small stuff-sack instead. Bertha will be disappointed that I'm not including any rings. They are, after all, the one component of wedding paraphernalia that can be worn again without causing a stir. I may give her the diamond from the ring Lynn gave me.

I remember a woman, a friend of auntie Jane's, dyeing her tulle wedding dress emerald green. Wearing it to a Christmas party. Waiting six months for her skin to shed the shade it left. I wonder about the shadow a white dress makes.

So far I've cast off the headpiece I wore when I married Domenic, the garters I wore at five weddings, the red veil I wore when I married Jack, and the missal I carried when I married Raj. I think Raj left me because the prayer book insulted his grandmother, but I'm not sure. I feel good about Lynn's vest. The man we met at Seebe will use it properly.

I've been home for three days and I manage to make two decisions: one about forks and the other about underskirts. I consider making a sail out of my Granny's underskirt, the only thing I wore when I married Joel that I can bear to part with, but the cotton is so thin I don't think it will trap air.

The answering machine plays back four messages from Nemit. Each reminds me of something related to Bertha's well-being. I erase the last without listening to what she says. Six people inquire about new river listings. I set up appointments for each that I'll keep the week after next. Five messages are from the designer who viewed the Inglewood house. I call and tell her I've decided to keep the property, rent it to another vendor. She's abusive. I tell her to have sex with her skinny husband and hang up.

≈≈≈

The first thing I notice when I get home is the absence of water in my yard. The lawn is firmer. I walk the fence line. Only the bike path is still covered in a thin liquid coat. The second thing I notice is the note taped to my patio door by the Rivers and Lakes man. He's been reassigned. Invites me to spend the weekend in his fire lookout. Includes an excellent map of how to reach him.

I turn my attention to a chart of the next stretch of river Bertha and I will paddle: Calgary to Carseland. Total distance, seventy-five kilometers. Overall river: Grade I. Rapids: Class I. Nemit will be ecstatic. I wonder why her messages don't say anything about her new lover?

Bertha will love this section of the trip. Weight is not an issue, nothing to portage. We may even use the generator. Too bad about the underskirt, my fishing rod would have made a great mast.

I make a note of items to add to our gear, write *dining tent and small folding table with stools*. I add *pillows and bug light*, thinking that Bertha will be pleased. I include *2 bottles Zinfandel,* chew the pencil. Bertha will pack the cooler, including two lunches, one supper, one breakfast, and a multitude of fatty snacks. I cringe when the metal surrounding the eraser touches a filling, scratch *chocolate* at the top of the list before going to bed. Heavy rain falls all night.

I sleep for three hours before I hear Bertha downstairs in my kitchen. I look at the clock: six forty-nine.

"Don't worry about the weather!" she says, as she throws the glass shower door open, bouncing it off the commode.

"Do you mind?"

She closes the door. One minute later I hear her peeing, her body a blurred mass through the marbled door. "The sun is breaking through, forecast is dry for the next three days," she says over the sound.

Chapter XVI

Nemit drives us to the southeast end of the city, leaves us at Bankside in Fish Creek Park. Adam is still in bed. She kisses Bertha full on the mouth, then rushes away to wake him for a ball game.

When the canoe is loaded and ready to go Bertha disappears into the vaulted Provincial building. I find her in the washroom. Rolls her lips in on themselves when she sees me.

"What's the matter?" I ask. Her hands are covered in dust. "I thought I had the last of Ed. Jesus Christ, Bertha."

"It broke in my pocket," she whimpers, suspends a baggie from one hand, tries to retain the contents in the other.

"It's okay, Bertha," I put my arm around her shoulder.

I walk at her side, hands under hers, through two doors, across a bike path, down a rough slope, across a grassy ledge to the river. I crouch and watch liquid replace ash in the plastic bag. Bertha sobs.

"I don't understand," I say. My brain records sensation as water burns my skin.

She shakes her head.

"Maybe you should keep the other one," I suggest. Contradictions. I think of the headwaters and Johnston Valley and Seebe and I still don't understand.

"Give me—some—some, t—time," she whispers.

≈≈≈

Bertha says nothing when we eddy out and make a rough turn into the current, nothing fifteen minutes later about my directions to stay to the middle of the left span of the Highway 22X bridge. She knows from our lessons on the Calgary stretch that we always navigate the center span. She says nothing about leaving the city limits. Paddles numbly where I tell her. I steer us almost perpendicular to the flow, into the tip zone. Let the bow swing downstream. No reaction. I maneuver us down a narrow weeded branch of river that grounds us in the Cottonwood Golf Course, near the clubhouse. She only reacts when the four men on the first tee take off their shoes and socks and wade in to help us.

"My daughter has a bad back," she manages, plants herself next to me instead of next to the striking looking gent with the tan and the silver hair. Doesn't complain about getting her feet wet up to her knees.

Six of us muscle the full canoe off the mud hump. The men laugh and wave at the woman on the bank who says, "Mind if we play through?" The men throw out their names as we paddle away, invite us to come in for a drink on the return trip.

"What the heck did you put us in there for?" Bertha asks, as we reach the main channel again.

"For fun!" I say.

"Some fun!" she says, grinning. "Play nice!"

At least she seems conscious now.

≈≈≈

I make a conscious decision, when I marry Thomas. Don't see him for years; have trouble remembering why I should recognize him when I see him standing next to Nemit in the lobby of an oil company office. Turns out they both work for the same giant. I hear an elevator, think it's a flute. Then I remember Thomas next to a frozen lake, his face ruddy and cold, my limbs Whitefish weak.

"My legs are asleep, Marlo," Bertha's voice interrupts. "Let's stop for a bit."

"Switch up to the seat, that'll help."

"I need to stop," she says.

I check the banks ahead. The Cliffs of Doom rise a hundred or so feet above us on one side. Looks like a brand new sport utility vehicle, roof crushed partway down the slope.

"There's a gravel bar up ahead. Draw right," I say.

Her knuckles shine white around the top of her paddle.

≈≈≈

Bertha's hands shake as she takes the top off the cooler.

I think she's in control, until this morning. She makes decisions based on what she thinks are sound reasons. She practises separation by degrees.

"I'm just going over here for a bit," she says. Wanders through a clump of poplar trees munching on mixed nuts and raisins.

When I separate from Thomas it's for sound reasons. He's protective and practical. He helps me disconnect from Lynn. He's well-prepared for the future.
He doesn't see the need to raise children. I leave him because he's habitual. I take part of the only wedding gift we accept: stainless steel flatware from Bertha and Ed. Forks. Tines scarred by his teeth. I hardly eat when we're together for meals. Can't stand the sound of enamel on steel.

"You should have some protein," Bertha says, when she comes back. "Give your body what it needs."

"My basic problem," I say. "Are you okay, Bertha?"

"Okay?"

"I mean you seem sort of—"

"Sort of what?"

"Quiet?"

"What were *you* thinking about all that time—besides hazards?"

"Thomas Phillips."

"Poor man was devastated when you left him. Quit his job and moved to the homestead. I think he's been down there ever since."

"He was ready to retire."

"He's what? Twelve years older than you?"

"Thirteen."

"You could have stopped working and sold the house in Bowness, and the Inglewood house, and just settled next to that little river. Lived off the income from your rental properties."

"Too dry and windy."

"He was very good to you, even did your laundry! How could you let a man like that go? I tried to talk to him. Too proud. Too close to my own age to imagine confiding in a woman."

A group of five heavily-laden canoes floats towards us. There's a single paddler in the lead canoe. Each of the others has two paddlers. One contains adults.

"Any trouble ladies?" the lead canoeist calls out.

"None!" I call back. "Must be an instructor from the Bow Waters Club or maybe from the University," I say to Bertha.

"Sounds Australian. Why didn't we get him?" She sounds like her old self.

"All right boys," he says, "back paddle—slowly Scott! With your partner Evan. Okay, spread out a bit. Sheila—you're too close to me."

"My name's not Sheila!" one of the paddlers calls.

"No mate, your name *is* Sheila when you can't get on a simple move like that one!"

The whole group laughs.

"They look about sixteen," Bertha says. "Great, just what we need."

"Okay blokes, remember how to ferry? We're now going upstream so that we can join those ladies on that nice bank over there for a bite of lunch."

There's low chatter as the boats huddle slightly downstream. They watch the instructor demonstrate the technique.

"Front ferry, boys! Stern in the current. Keep the angle shallow, don't let the current," he paddles with more effort, "take the bow straight, or you'll just—go downstream. Notice I'm paddling forward, Sheila."

The group cheers when he raises his baseball cap to us.

"Show-off," Bertha says. "That wasn't so hard."

"Boy scouts," he winks at me. "Run for your lives."

He paddles slightly downstream of the group and hovers in the middle. "First canoe!" he calls. "Let's go, Scotty!"

"Good idea," Bertha says. "Let's go."

"Don't you want to watch?"

"Not really. One boy is fine, but six plus the leaders plus the instructor? That's a small herd."

We pull on our life-jackets. I sit in the stern while Bertha pushes us out and hops in.

"Catch up with you later," the instructor drawls, as we paddle past.

"I hope not," Bertha says, switching sides.

"Pivot turn!" I call.

"Oh, for God's sake," she says, but she knows the move and draws on the starboard side while I draw on the port side. We complete the spin. I wave to the instructor who laughs and we head down the Bow toward its confluence with the Highwood.

≈≈≈

No crows on this stretch of river. I was amazed the first time I paddled to Carseland. Couldn't stop taking photographs of the birds: great flocks of pelican and stork standing in the shallows, covering whole islands. Hard to imagine the dry towns and highways perched out of sight on the prairie above. Only lush vegetation here. There is one stretch of cabins, dubbed "The Mansion Run" below Indus. Arranged for three sales there. Been on this trip eight times and have never seen people in those places. Some ranches border the river, but few campgrounds, and powerboats are rare.

We pass two float boats and four silent fly-fishermen, chest high waders keeping their red plaid shirts dry. I wonder if the shirts are standard issue by the tour company, or if they come free with their expensive hats. Bertha blows them a kiss.

"Ma'am—little ma'am," the fifth one says.

"How much you think a weekend of resting line on the water costs?" Bertha asks.

"Don't know."

"Joel's dad still runs that outfitter's cabin on the Highwood. Reason he couldn't come to your wedding," she says, "remember?"

"I remember. Didn't trust me. Afraid his land would end up in my hands. Willed it to Joel. Afraid because I didn't want kids."

"What about his wife?"

"Bypassed her completely."

"But how could he do that? I mean legally, isn't it *theirs?* The marital home? Where would she live if he died?"

"Completely up to the son. Made her sign something before they married. Light years ahead of his contemporaries. Probably designed the prenuptial agreement Joel brought to me. Land's been in the family since the great-grandfather came over from Stirling."

"Good thing that Joel likes his mother."

"Joel's from a run of men who were property heavy."

"Property heavy—now that would be you."

"I still believe that investing in land is the best thing a woman can do. Every husband but Domenic signed away his right to my business. When I married Dom I didn't own a thing. When I came home after my post-pubescent adventure, I still didn't own anything."

"Ed thought Domenic was too young for you. I thought you were in love."

I'm surprised that my conversation with my mother ends here. Whether she responds to me or not, she has the power to punctuate the conversation, speak in tongues, hold me at wordpoint. Do you ever wonder why you defer to your mother? It's not her knowledge or intellect, or her personal strength, or even her voice that establishes her rule. It's the annoying way that she knows you better than you know yourself. Does she know you because you are a small part of the whole that she was? The part of herself that she allows to escape from the birth canal into the main stream? Is the process of heredity involuntary? Or is the body of the mother in control of the process, like the one the egg uses to draw the millions of already dying sperm toward her? After she manages ejaculation and fertilization, does the mother send physical nourishment through the umbilical chord? Or does the embryo take what she needs?

"We're eating lunch now!" Bertha startles me. "I was wondering when you'd blink," she says over her shoulder. "What's the key to choosing a place?"

"Anywhere that you think looks good," I reply.

She chooses well. Spots an eddy on the left where there's a small strip of damp earth and a six-inch step up to a grassy ledge. We go in bow first. Bertha draws left, cross bow as the front leaves the current. I draw right and the stern swings around so that we face upstream. She's relaxed and doesn't seem to mind the small jolt the canoe makes when it crosses the eddy line.

"I think I'd like to try steering next," she says. "Today may be my only chance."

Bertha has taken the time to prepare before we leave. Lunch is fish wrapped in parchment packets. She takes the paper bundles from a plastic box and bakes them in a deep skillet, lid on, over the stove.

"You told me no restrictions and this lunch is light." She thinks my face shows scorn instead of surprise, hands me a plastic wine glass.

"It's fabulous!" I say. "Gourmet! What's for dinner?"

"Our last supper will be cranberry pork tenderloin, new potatoes roasted in a Dijon paste, vegetable medley, and pie."

"Pie?"

"I read up on reflector ovens," she says.

We're enjoying the fresh tomatoes, red and yellow peppers and seasoned halibut, sipping Pinot Blanc when the scout group floats past, their canoes tied together like a large raft. The adults and the instructor snooze. Four boys paddle from the outside corners. The centamaran turns large slow circles midstream.

"Sleep," I say. "What a good idea."

When I awake, Bertha writes in a journal. I lie on my back, life-jacket under my head, watching. I don't want to take the moment away from her. I had no idea that she ever wrote anything down. Her pen seems to dent the page and
I feel as if I am eavesdropping.

I stretch and yawn but she stays focused on the hard cover book. I crawl to the canoe and take out my camera case. Two shots left on the black and white roll. I capture the intensity on her face with the first and zoom out to include her whole body with the second. "Mother Below Tree," I think as the film rewinds. How does she classify me on the pages of that journal? Perhaps I do not appear at all.

She closes the book and says, "I have one last thing to do before I'll be ready to leave."

She puts the journal in her clothes bag and takes out a trowel, tries to dig near the tree she sat under.

"Here, let me help."

I slice into the earth with my knife perpendicular to the surface several times, loosen the tangle of wild grass, rip out the stalks.

She scrapes a hole in the ground that has no particular dimensions, trickles the last of Ed's ashes into the space. We use our hands to cover the ashes with dirt.

She holds up the small stuff-sack. "What will you do with the forks?"

I take two, stick the tines in the earth, and let the handles rest together. They form a triangle with the surface of the ground. I lash a small wavy branch to the sharp angle at the top, using half of the drawstring from the stuff sack.

Bertha sings one verse of, "The Lord is My Shepherd," before she makes the sign of the cross and stands up, rosary in her hand.

"I prayed for entrance into heaven," she says, touches the crucifix to her eyes and her lips.

I can't answer. My throat constricts and my face is wet. Stays that way no matter that I swab my tears with the backs of both hands. I think about devotion.

"That Joel's Saint Christopher you're wearing?" she asks.

≈≈≈

"J-stroke," I say from the bow of the canoe. "Your paddle is the rudder." The canoe is off centre in the middle of the river.

Bertha laughs and I do a cross bow draw to straighten us out.

"Why the Saint Christopher?" she asks.

"Patron saint of travel."

"Think something's going to happen?"

"No," I say. "Not unless you don't level us out."

"I can't quite get the feel of the stroke," she says.

"Persevere! Turn your hand over so your thumb turns in and down at the end of the stroke."

"But then I'll pry."

"Then you'll pry," I say. "There aren't any rapids to worry about so unless we are sideways on a rock, I'm not concerned about falling in."

She does try, tries for a good kilometre or so.

"Not working."

"Okay, we'll just paddle straight on opposite sides, but we'll have to switch every ten strokes to stay—in the middle."

After three quarters of an hour of zigzagging, we pull out and change positions. I don't want Bertha to be at the helm when we reach the Highwood. No significant rapids there but the standing waves must be negotiated head on. Each river folds in on the other at the conjunction, like smooth ingredients suspended in a mixing bowl.

≈≈≈

I wonder how it feels when you defer to your daughter. Maybe it's like separating the yolk from the egg using only your fingers. Are you frustrated? Happy or sad with the outcome? You can't hold on to the contents of the shell. Can you separate the fluid mass without bursting the yolk?

Bertha once told me that she was jealous. I think she was about fifty-nine at the time. Said she felt as if her body was falling apart. Constantly compared her body to my body. Made public note of the fact that mine was in its prime, tried to dress like me, tried to run with me. Couldn't keep up. I'd been training for a marathon for six months. She cried when I left her panting a third of the way up Home Road. I forced myself to jog slowly all the way back along the river while she sulked. Ed scowled at me for not being more considerate.

"Do you think Ed is happy where he is?" Bertha asks.

"Happy?"

"You know, content."

"Where is he exactly? I don't think I know."

"In heaven, of course. He didn't lead a bad life, so he can't be in hell. Didn't take his own life, so he can't be in purgatory."

"I wonder how long it really takes to die."

"Don't, Marlo. I wonder how long you have to stay in purgatory."

"How long does it take to separate the mind from the body?"

"I was afraid of being buried alive as a kid."

"Haven't you ever wondered how many levels of unconsciousness there are before the brain doesn't function?"

"When I'm dead, promise to pinch me?"

"Under your arms or your chin?"

"Both!" she says. "I believe that if the dead have something to say to us, they'll find ways."

"As in, as a ghost?"

"As in, won't leave us until they are ready whether they are enclosed in a body or not."

"I think you're reaching," I say.

"I couldn't find Ed's ring this weekend."

"Couldn't find his ring?

"Couldn't find his ring. And you know how long it's been on the bedside."

"Did you find it?"

"Yes I found it."

"Where?"

"In my pocket."

"You must have put it there, and forgotten."

"This pocket," she says, motioning to the Velcro topped version on the front of her life-jacket.

I think she's losing her mind.

"I hear loud water!"

"Don't panic, Bertha. We're coming up on the Highwood."

"Tell me I won't need to get wet!"

"The water is much warmer here!"

"That's so comforting," she says, as we begin to bounce through the waves.

"Campsite—second—island on the—left."

≈≈≈

Bertha wears Ed's ring on the thumb of her left hand. Busies herself inside the dining tent. Sets the small tabletop. The pie she constructed at home sits on top of the cooler in an old stoneware dish. I can't believe she's going to such great lengths. The fire is burning strong and the four-sided open metal cube that she says is an oven is cooking pork tenderloin and potatoes. Looks like the end of a heating duct.

"Twenty-five minutes," she says. "Make sure we don't run out of wood."

I trace my way through the stand of skinny poplar and birch in the middle of our island, stand on the bank of the shaded narrow channel that divides us from the nearest ranch. On the map we're between the towns of Indus and Langdon. I walk downstream checking the far end of the island for the scout group. They've made a giant shelter with the canoes and a series of tarps. One tent stands at least fifty feet back from the canoe structure and a cocoon hammock is suspended between two trees where I emerge.

"G'day," says a voice from behind the mesh.

"Hi!" I say back. "How small does that contraption pack?"

"To about the size of a water bottle, my lovely," the instructor says, slipping out between the nylon bottom and the bug net.

"Thought your group might have camped at McKinnon Flats."

"Naw—too many other people there. Usually no one else on this island."

"I know," I reply.

"Jake," he says, extending his hand.

"Marlo," I say. "Come and visit us later. Got to get back."

≈≈≈

I hear Bertha's voice in conversation as I come full-circle to our camp. When I get closer I see the blue hull of an overturned kayak crowned by a spray skirt. I should have known. I drop the wood by the fire next to another pile that Bertha must have asked Joel to collect. She never gives up.

"In the neighborhood?" I ask.

"Sort off," he says, laughing. "Just tripping down to the flats from Dad's place. Bertha said you two'd be here. Thought I'd check up on you."

"And how does everything look?" I ask, hands on my hips.

"Fine," he says, sipping chocolate from a steaming cup that Bertha hands him.

"Didn't know we were having company," I say to her.

"Thought I'd make it a surprise."

"Well I've invited someone too," I say, as if I'm thirteen. "The scouts are at the other end of the island."

≈≈≈

Bertha and Joel eat and joke as if we're sitting at the dining room table at home and Ed has abandoned us to finish up something he's building in the garage. I sit on the cooler, eat in complete silence, unsure of myself and of what I'll say if I let myself go.

Joel tells Bertha that his sister just gave birth to a son.

I down my third cup of wine. "That's great," I say. "Now your Dad won't have to worry about his land."

And then we are twelve. The scout group finds us just as Bertha decides that the pie is ready. She divides it into chunks and the boys file past her with their troop cups outstretched as if collecting alms. I delight in telling them to keep the forks, which I pull one by one from the stuff sack. The boys chew and maw the tines long after the pie is devoured, seem to know by instinct what to do with the metal. My teeth cringe as I watch. The leaders admire the "oven," which Bertha explains in great detail while the instructor works to hold my attention with stories of the Nahanni River.

"Excuse me," I say, when I see Joel pulling on his thin yellow gloves and stepping through the rubber spray skirt. "Have to leave so soon?"

"Dad's picking me up in about twenty minutes. I want to be off the river before dark."

"Well tell him I say hello and tell Christine I say congrats. Should take you less than ten minutes to get from here to McKinnon flats."

I try to focus on the conversation that Bertha has with Joel as he holds the kayak over his head and walks toward the river. Try to listen to his answer to her question about partners, mouth, *Bye*, when he turns, let the instructor fill my cup with more wine.

≈≈≈

"You could have told me that you'd invited him!" I say to Bertha later. The generator hums, the light outside cracks with dying bugs, and Bertha's little stereo plays pipe music.

"You could have told me about the damn scouts!" she fires back. "You're drunk." She turns the music off.

"So what. I've had a long day." I have no idea how many glasses I've consumed, but I remember opening the second bottle. "Going to pass judgment on me now? Lecture me about what a *good* husband Joel would've been? Tell me that I didn't *have* to marry all those other men?"

"Give me a cup, will you?"

"Well I have no excuse!" I say, passing her one. "Except that I've been brainwashed."

"Brainwashed?" she asks, draining the bottle.

"What Nemit says—since birth—to buy into the most widely popular brand in the world."

"I don't follow."

"The wife brand."

"Like on a cow?"

"No, but maybe we can patent that idea, turn it into a subliminal sign and sell it to some of the ranchers around here. Let them burn it into the hides of their calves. Then we can have the last laugh."

"I think you've had way too much." She tries to take my cup, but I hug it to my chest. Spill half of the contents on my fleece. "I think you're cynical," she continues. "Look at Ed and me. We've been together practically all our lives. 'Till now." She drinks. "Today people think they can change partners whenever they want, throw someone away like an out-of-fashion pair of jeans."

"It's catch twenty-two and you know it."

"What *are* you talking about?"

"Don't be coy with me, Bertha. You know exactly what I mean. When you wear a ring there's always someone looking to see how big it is, or ask you where you live, or what your husband does. And when you don't have a husband—"

"People think you're a threat—"

"Exactly!"

"Don't trust you around their husbands and sons."

"That's happened to you?" I spill wine on the ground trying to center my weight on the three-legged stool.

"Since Ed passed. Almost immediately. The Tai Chi wives don't want me too close. Betty next door actually thinks I *like* her scrawny Stan, and Jane, my own sister, looks at me sideways when her drunk of a son is around."

"Let's have more wine," I say.

"That's the end of the two bottles of Zin," she says. "Can't believe you're not passed out."

I throw my hands up. "Everyone either wants to be a wife, or to have one. Who thought up the idea? It's fucking brilliant!"

I remember laying my head on the table, but not how I get into my sleeping bag or how I take off my pants.

≈≈≈

I wake up struggling against what I think is a veil. It's the wall of the dining tent. I'm completely off the Thermarest that Bertha must have brought in here for me. The smell of coffee and bannock weighs me down.

"How do you feel?"

I cradle my head in my arms as two ultra-lights fly overhead. They sound like my neighbor's lawn mower. Bertha jumps up and down and waves.

"I see you Joel! I see you Fred! Marlo! Marlo!" she shrieks. "Look at them!"

"I am definitely not selling the house to Joel. He can damn well rent it!"

"Come on! You're going to miss them!"

"You're burning the bannock," I manage, as I roll into a ball.

I zip my sleeping bag up from the foot and stumble outside, hood over my head. Bertha throws the skillet on the grass and turns off the one-burner stove.

"Here they come!" she calls. "I wish I'd tried flying! Look! Look!"

The drone builds to a whine and then a loud buzz. They seem dangerously close to the treetops. This time one of the pilots dips a wing and drops a huge water balloon near the canoe.

"Did you see that? Did you?" She runs toward me from the riverbank. "He sure went to a lot of trouble," she says, as the drone fades. "I miss him already. Don't you?"

"Not really," I lie, as I sit on the ground.

She's already collapsed and packed the tent. Her canoe bag, the table and the stools, the generator, the bug light, her stereo, the reflector oven, and my camera case are all stacked neatly waiting to be loaded.

"Nemit and Adam will have to wait if we don't start soon," she says. "I'll make some more bannock. You'll feel better after we absorb some of that stomach acid. Here's something for your head."

She hands me two pills and a water bottle full of freezing water.

"That river water?" I ask.

I swallow the pills dry and pour the water over my head.

She natters about Joel and how he's promised to look after me when she's gone, doesn't stop. Insists on brushing out my hair. I tolerate the strokes, skin pulling away from my eyes with every draw of the brush. I let her make a long braid, remember the time she broke a hairbrush over my head when I wouldn't stay still. I think I was seven.

Her voice echoes when I go into the trees to squat. I think I hear another motor, imagine Joel hovering, waiting for me to let go.

≈≈≈

The boy scouts are landed at McKinnon flats when we paddle by. Jake calls, "You're numba—you didn't give me your numba!"

"You're not!" Bertha says, looking back.

I manage a grin. I can't wait to get off the water. Can't wait for the silence of alone to engulf me, comfort me, soothe me. This last section of river is tedious and slow and ever branching. Branching left and left and left to avoid the weir. Branching towards the dirt road that winds down from the cliffs near Carseland.

Have you ever noticed how slowly deep water moves? Deceptively calm. I lie on top of the gear while Bertha paddles in the bow. It's hot. I dream that my mother and I cliff-jump; imagine the white of her legs and the red of her suit above me as I sink. I hold my breath, wake after my lungs fill with water, flailing and coughing.

"Have you ever noticed how deeply you sleep?" my mother asks. "Deceptively calm. Who were you fighting off this time? We're nearly at the end, you know." Her voice is so quiet I can barely make out the words.

I wipe drool from my chin and think about the beginning, about the headwaters, about the noise, about the rushing white water. Our surroundings are tranquil, quiet. I think about the riverbed, about the elements lifting and moving below us, about the flow that carries us.

I squint up at the back of my mother's head and see reluctance in the pink skin below the tufts of her hair. She turns when my paddle clunks against the gunwale, kneels when I shift my weight from the gear to my seat.

I take frequent breaks, paddle without meaning.

Bertha prays. Wraps the rosary around her wrist—it hits her paddle. Sets the rosary on her thigh—it slides to her feet. She puts down her paddle and picks up the crucifix. I watch as she touches the cross to her ears.

"It's going to get shallow soon," I say. "I'll need you to stroke."

I steer us into the last left-branching channel.

The cross touches the end of her nose. Before she takes up her paddle she turns and looks through me, crucifix pressed between her palms. Puts the beads in the pocket on her life-jacket next to Ed's ring, paddles without stopping without talking without saying until we reach the final bend.

As we enter the sharp elbow of river that defines the pull out, I decide that she hates endings. The river curves three hundred feet away from the main stream. We land the canoe bow-first. My feet sink in the soft mud as I get out and hold onto the stern. There's fifty yards of hard packed dirt between us and the gravel track that divides the portage area. It conceals the observation point, and the launch further downstream.

Bertha looks up at the edge of the prairie, sways as she stands on the bank holding the bow rope. Dust moves behind Nemit's car as it crawls down the steep slope, drives on the raised road in front of us. We pull the canoe part way out of the water. She leaves the gravel and parks.

"Mom's already been here twice." Adam jumps out and slams the passenger door.

"Thought I was in the wrong place," Nemit says through her open window. "Drove back up the hill and over to Wyndham Provincial Park. No one fishing here or there said they'd seen you. I've been worrying!" She hugs me hard, shoulders and arms reaching through the doorframe.

Bertha stands back from us, Ed's ring on her thumb, rosary like a bracelet, life-jacket on the ground.

I waddle back and forth between the canoe and the car, dripping dry sweat and dropping gear that Nemit loads behind the back seat.

"Where's Adam?" Bertha asks. "Where's Adam?"

"He's looking at the weir," Nemit tells her gently.

"Is that safe?"

"There's a fence only a monkey could climb," I tell her quietly. I try to rub her back but she maneuvers out of reach. I press my hand against my head in the place where the pills have worn off.

Bertha walks past the car, crosses the raised road, and disappears in the direction of the observation deck.

"Something's wrong," Nemit, whispers.

"She's stiff with the effort and the stress," I say. "Been quiet most of the day. Maybe it's just the finality of what she's done. She buried the last of Ed yesterday." I fold an empty canoe bag and hand it to her.

"Bertha's not a young woman," Nemit scolds. She tucks the yellow bag behind the spare wheel. "I'm going to check on Adam."

I wade into the shallow water and reach for the last of the gear. *Maybe a wee prayer'll help?* I wince, pick up the cooler and pull it across the gunwale.

≈≈≈

"You okay?" I ask Bertha when she comes back ten minutes later. "Want to sit in the car while I wash the outside of the canoe?"

"I'm fine, perfectly fine," she says. "Go get the other two and I'll finish."

She opens her canoe bag, peers in the top, worms a hand towards the bottom. I think she just needs a few minutes.

≈≈≈

Nemit, Adam, and I watch two men cast lines in the river a few hundred feet from the base of the weir. I turn and look toward the launch. "Maybe we should have gone further."

"I don't think so," Nemit replies.

"All the way to the South Saskatchewan."

"Why?"

"To ease this letting go process."

Adam stands on the cement wall, leans into the steel mesh that rises twenty feet in the air, hands on the steel uprights which are about a foot apart. "That a keeper?"

The low line of colored buoys that span the river above the weir dance in the constant rush and draft. "That's a keeper," I say. "Come on down."

I start walking back to the car, unable to resist the voice that whispers, *Run lassie!* I sprint. Adam and Nemit think I'm teasing and join in, make it a race.

We hear the fishermen yelling as we reach the road. The pain in my throat is severe. My legs are numb. Something touches me square between the shoulder blades where my braid ends. Bertha and the canoe are gone. I walk, shoulders high, arms stiff, towards the car. My parents' wedding rings rest on the dash. I pick them up, make a fist.

I run back, over the road, past the observation deck, and down the slope on the other side. I skid to a stop near the two men. One is on his knees; the other is yelling obscenities into a cell phone. I pay dearly to replace the graphite rods they drop in the river when the woman wearing the blue pillbox hat disappears below the surface.

Chapter XVII

I meet Joel at the Inglewood house. Discuss the terms of the purchase agreement I bring with me. He's impressed by the keyless entry system, immediately disarms the line to the security firm.

He signs after scanning the pages, talks about filling the planters and settling into the old map room. He climbs the metal stairs that we built with Ed's welding gear. We sit on the floor at the top, bodies inches from engagement.

I choose that location to deliver Bertha's letter. The stairs absorb his emotions for three hours. Takes another two before he gains even a semblance of composure. He tells me that the letter is a confession. He reads Bertha's words again and again.

I examine the face that neither looks for nor expects an embrace. My hands shake in proximity to his. He doesn't ask why.

≈≈≈

When I read Bertha's diary I am surprised by what I find. Each entry begins: *Dear Marlo...Have you ever noticed...* The first is dated the day after Ed dies and the last the night before she dies. I take in the final sentences and wonder how she imagined herself dead.

I feel a great sadness, but not sadness wrought with tears. The police psychologist suggests that I deal with the pain and the guilt I might feel, and deal with it soon. I feel no guilt. I realize that my mother was more in love with the idea of property than I am. I didn't understand until now. Remarkable and fantastic. Her death is not romantic; there is no exchange, no engagement between. What she *was* is dead—only present now in half-remembered events and in the stories Nemit tells. Bertha made a decision, I won't dream an ending based on what I think she believed. I'll think of another beginning.

≋≋≋

Nemit dreams of my mother's love. Wanders through Bertha's house as I pack her belongings, calls her *Angel*, fingers porcelain statues with wings that Bertha labeled with her name. Enthralls me, asks if she might give them away. I suggest the nuns at Saint Bernard's.

A note on top of the *Car and Driver* wall instructs me to recycle the magazines but to keep the paperback that Granda loved so much. Nemit takes the stack to Adam's school. Leaves me sitting in a teak chair where the whirlpool used to be, clutching the novel and a letter directing me to speak with Father Joe.

My mother left instructions for me at the church. The last time we attended mass she asked the parish priest to keep her will. A sealed envelope with my name on it contains the title to her house, directions to four bags of ashes, and two requests. One: cremate my body. Two: combine my ashes with Ed's. She never let my father go in the river, except by pure accident the day we began the trip to Carseland.

I expect my mother often, anticipate her voice on Sunday mornings and nurture her love of beginnings.

Wissenschaftlicher Buchverlag bietet

kostenfreie

Publikation

von

wissenschaftlichen Arbeiten

Diplomarbeiten, Magisterarbeiten, Master und Bachelor Theses
sowie Dissertationen, Habilitationen und wissenschaftliche Monographien

Sie verfügen über eine wissenschaftliche Abschlußarbeit zu aktuellen oder zeitlosen
Fragestellungen, die hohen inhaltlichen und formalen Ansprüchen genügt,
und haben **Interesse an einer honorarvergüteten Publikation**?

Dann senden Sie bitte erste Informationen über Ihre Arbeit per Email
an info@vdm-verlag.de. Unser Außenlektorat meldet sich umgehend bei Ihnen.

VDM Verlag Dr. Müller Aktiengesellschaft & Co. KG
Dudweiler Landstraße 125a
D - 66123 Saarbrücken

www.vdm-verlag.de